QUEEN'S TREASURE

I0571596

Copyright © A.E. Stewart 2016

Published by A.E. Stewart

*Cover artwork by Gary Taaffe, Copyright © A.E. Stewart 2016
Formatting by Gary Taaffe, Copyright © A.E. Stewart 2016*

*Names, characters, places and incidents are either products of the
author's imagination or are used fictitiously.*

The moral right of the author has been asserted

ISBN: 978-0-9923796-8-1

*Gary Taaffe
BunyaPublishing.com
BunyaPublishing@gmail.com*

Titles available in the
SILVER THIEVES
series
(in reading order)

QUEEN'S TREASURE

A CROOK'S TREASURE

SAHARAN TREASURE

TINAN HINAN

Book 1

QUEEN'S TREASURE

A.E. STEWART

BUNYA
PUBLISHING.com

PART ONE

— CHAPTER ONE —

Cook's Spoon

Australia 1770

Jack ran down the narrow cobbled streets as fast as his stocky legs could carry him. The press gang was after him and he had no desire to go to sea as a volunteer or otherwise. He slipped into a dark alley, caught his breath and waited for silence. When the sound of running footsteps had ceased, he peeped out. Unfortunately for Jack the moon was full and visibility was excellent. Just as he was about to retreat, he felt two strong hands locked around his throat. That was the last thing that he recalled before waking up with a sore head on a rocking ship. He was given clean clothes and a hammock, the value of which would be deducted from his wages on return to port. He was taken to the galley where he met another young man called Billy Smith who had also been 'pressed.'

Billy who had always lived by his wits, stealing and evading the law was a tall, skinny youth with sallow skin and a crooked grin. He never knew his parents, and had existed on a near starvation diet, growing up in the streets and alleyways. His change of life was a big improvement for him.

Their job was to help the cook prepare food for the Officers Mess as well as for Captain Cook who usually ate alone in his Great Cabin.

Jack Christie was born in Plymouth to a poor family. His mother died giving him birth so Jack was left in the hands of his father and a kindly woman next door who took care of him as best she could. His father was a dockyard worker who had to walk to work every day. Their simple home was situated close to Plymouth Dock where an older Jack found himself with time on his hands and little to do. Jack was not tall or even good looking, but he had an infectious smile and a ready wit. Just living so close to the port, unemployed and idle, he was ripe for the picking and an introduction to a complete change of life.

When a ship was in port and short of men, some of the ship's crew was sent ashore and formed into press gangs. This meant that a man could be forced against his will to serve on board any King's ship that happened to need men. Once a man had been seized by the press gang, he was offered a choice: sign up as a volunteer and receive the benefits or remain 'pressed' and receive nothing. Apprentices who carried written proof called 'Protections' were exempt from being pressed.

The Endeavour had left Plymouth in 1768 to observe the transit of Venus across the sun and to seek evidence of the "unknown Southern land."

Its Captain, James Cook was an intelligent man of superior character. From humble beginnings, the son of a poor serving man, he was known as a trustworthy and cheerful individual. He willingly enlisted in the Royal Navy as his mind was decidedly inclined towards the sea, and he thought it wiser to do this rather than be hauled against his will by the press gangs.

Sailing after the examination of the shores of New Zealand, Cook turned west and after three weeks came in sight of the coast of New Holland. At ten o'clock on the 11th. June 1770, Cook had his first disaster. It was a fine moonlit night and he had retired to bed when without any warning a shudder was felt and the ship heeled over.

Jack heard the crashing of objects in the galley as he swung out of his hammock and nudged Billy to wake up.

'Hey Billy, something is amiss. This ship is listing badly, and it seems stuck. We had better go and see if we can help.'

Billy was not keen to go as he was still tired after cleaning the plates and cutlery from the night's dinner, but Jack was insistent. When they arrived on deck, all was a bustling scene as they eyed the capstans manned as orders were given to lighten her. Six cannon, casks, chains and other stuff were dumped overboard. At noon the tide had dropped and the sea was perfectly calm, but too short to re-float her. All were waiting anxiously for the midnight tide to arrive, and at nine p.m. the vessel lurched and suddenly righted itself. She rode the rising swell, with the pumps being furiously manned to the point of near exhaustion for the men involved. Jack looked around for Billy to take his turn, but he was nowhere to be seen. He uttered a curse.

'Damn his eyes. Where is he? Just when he's needed, he disappears.'

Billy had hurried below decks heading for the Captain's Great Cabin. With all the turmoil going on up top, Billy was sure that he could enter unnoticed. Normally a guard was stationed outside, but not at the moment. He quickly found what he was seeking. It was a large silver spoon. Billy had cleaned and polished it so often, admiring his distorted reflection, that he could remember by heart the quaint little marked boxes engraved on the underneath side. Carefully stowing it into his blouse, he hurried below decks to hide it.

Kissing it quickly, he whispered. 'Rest here my lovely I've got plans for you.'

The night of near tragedy left Jack close to exhaustion, and they were not out of danger yet. The pumps and the men were working at a dangerous pace. A sail had been placed under the ship to cling to the hole made by the collision and the ship had to be beached and repaired. Billy was fortunate that the missing spoon had gone unnoticed during all the chaos and confusion, but he made sure that he retrieved it from its hiding place when the journey ended.

After two years Cook returned to England. Despite his shattered crew and a damaged ship, he was acclaimed for the great results from this voyage. Jack and Billy went their separate ways. Jack rose in the ranks of the Navy. His time spent on the Endeavour and the facts learned from Captain Cook were invaluable. (It was here that he was shown how the effects of scurvy can debilitate an otherwise healthy man). Cook insisted that the men eat sauerkraut to overcome the lack of fresh green vegetables, together with a committed regime of exercise to keep a sound mind and body.

Back then Billy and Jack had come through unscathed, but many did not. After sailing from Batavia, seven men died from a fever, and despite some shore leave whilst the ship was in for repairs, this was a long and eventful voyage. The count was finally recorded at twenty three deceased.

The loss of the American colonies in 1776 ushered in a new attitude towards a more humane tolerance of criminals in England. This was seen by some to be the result of a poor social system so a fresh start in life became an idea advocated by some philanthropists. In 1783 a bill was passed by Parliament to transport offenders to a 'place beyond the sea.' Many came to Australia, some never made it. Some were born on ship and some arrived only to be faced with starvation and hostility from the natives who rightfully did not appreciate their country being invaded.

By 1791 things had greatly improved as the ships brought more settlers as well as seeds to be sown for future crops. Both Billy and Jack were close to forty years of age. Billy had come to New South Wales as a Free Settler, hoping to make a fresh start in a new land.

Meanwhile, back in England, a certain John Macarthur saw the possibilities that the grazing lands in Australia had to offer for sheep and cattle, and he put energy and commitment into this project. When he arrived in the colony, he advertised for strong hands to help his new industry. Billy applied and was successful. He worked hard and prospered alongside Macarthur, who asked Billy to accompany him back to England in 1801. Macarthur's quest was for land and convicts to help his growing empire. After some wrangling with the Privy Council, he was at last granted five thousand acres.

When Billy was dining with Macarthur in London, they were joined by another couple who were introduced as Lord and Lady Christie. (Jack Christie had received a peerage after showing courage and leadership during the naval battle and defeat of the French Fleet in the West Indies in 1782). When he laid eyes on Billy, Jack Christie looked as if he had seen a ghost.

'By Jove, Billy is that really you?'

Billy knew that the last time that he had seen Jack was when they had served under Captain Cook together. Conversation was a little difficult as Billy's thoughts kept returning to the ship and the theft of the silver Spoon, but John Macarthur kept them all enthralled describing his enthusiastic plans for the wool industry in Australia.

Macarthur told Lord and Lady Christie that he would be pleased to show them both the wonderful sheep he was breeding and the production of fine wool that was the envy of many other countries. He extended an invitation for them to come to Australia. The evening ended with Jack promising Macarthur that he would think it over and inform him by the next mail ship of his decision.

The letter never came, but Jack and his two sons did. John Macarthur was pleasantly surprised on hearing of Lord Christie's arrival. Jack explained that he had retired from the Navy to attend his ailing wife. She had passed away, but not before she encouraged her husband and their two sons to make the voyage.

The years went by. John Macarthur died in 1834 after establishing the most wonderful enterprise that ever blessed Australia. Not long after Billy who was now a widower also succumbed to ill health, but he had one important thing that he wanted to do. He asked Jack to visit him. Seated alone before the fire in his country house, he welcomed Jack and asked him to pour some whisky into two crystal tumblers. Billy stared into the fire before taking a good swallow.

'Jack, my days are numbered and as I was not blessed with any children. I have no heirs to whom I can leave my fortune. Do you remember that night when the Endeavour hit the coral reef, and all hell broke loose? You tried to find me to help pump the ship as she was taking water?'

'Yes,' said Jack, 'I remember it well. It was a terrible night. Even though we managed to free the ship, everyone was exhausted.'

'That's right,' mumbled Billy. 'When you did find me, I had just left the Captain's Great cabin.'

'What? Why were you in there? Jack's frown deepened. Billy tipped up his whisky glass and handed it to Jack.

'Another one please Jack, I'm going to need it.' Billy's voice became a little stronger.

'You must remember the awful conditions that we had to endure on that long and ill fated voyage. The food that was only fit for the weevils which thrive in it, and the meat when we got it, was hard as leather and indigestible. If it wasn't for the regular tots of alcohol, I would have given up the ghost as some of those unlucky blighters did.'

He took the glass from Jack and asked him to pick up a cushion which was on the armchair.

'Jack inside that cushion's pocket you will find a little drawstring bag made of strong calico. It hasn't been opened for years, but now I am asking you to do this for me.'

Jack did as he was instructed and looked nonplussed as he removed an old silver serving spoon.

'I don't understand. Why are you keeping this hidden?'

'Don't you recognise it? It was the one that was used when the Captain dined on board the Endeavour.'

'I still don't understand how you come to have it,' Jack replied.

'When we struck that coral reef I thought that we were done for. I didn't care that the sailors were exhausted trying to keep the pumps ahead of the water intake, and I wouldn't have cared if the dammed ship had foundered. I went to his cabin and took the spoon, thinking that if we have to jump ship, I'm taking something of value with me. When we docked in England, it was easy to walk off with it inside my shirt. I intended to sell it, but couldn't bring myself to part with the only beautiful thing that I have ever possessed.'

Jack sighed at his own recollection of those days. He had a very different perspective, as he truly admired Captain Cook, and tried to emulate him in his own career. Looking a little closer at the spoon he noticed that it was engraved with the initials 'J.C.'

Billy continued. 'I want you to have something of value which means so much to me. We both shared that life together and this spoon is a symbol of that. It is just a co-incidence that his initials were the same as yours but even more fitting now. I want you to have it because you are the man that I always wished that I could be.'

Jack's throat had suddenly become dry.

'Yes my old shipmate, I will treasure it, and pass it onto my eldest son John with the story of how it has bound two old sailors together and the high esteem that I will always hold for it.' He leaned over and shook Billy's hand.

'Thank you Billy, I will let myself out.'

That was the last meeting between the two men. Shortly afterwards Billy passed away. Jack would sometimes take it out of the bag to give it a shine with a soft cloth, but he could not bring himself to use the spoon. He owned a fabulous canteen of silver cutlery for use on special occasions but he never forgot his humble beginnings and he never forgot Billy either.

COOK'S SPOON

When Jack's life ended, his eldest son John inherited the family's assets. The old spoon stayed in the linen press in the same bag for another generation. For nearly fifty years it lay amongst the linen in the cupboard at Christie House. Occasionally the staff would clean the bottom shelves out when the linen needed repairing or replacing, but the calico bag was pushed to the back on the top shelf and remained undisturbed there.

Both of Jack's sons were grown men. John managed to fritter away much of his inherited assets. His father left the house to John but he couldn't be bothered to maintain it and it soon fell into disrepair. John's younger brother Julian, moved into a small cottage with his wife in Parramatta. Over a glass of claret John told his brother that he was thinking of returning to England to live and that he wanted to see what the 'old country' was like. This did not surprise Julian.

Julian arrived home later that night with the good news.

'Mary my dear, how would you like to move out of this little cottage and into the family home? John is leaving Australia and he wants us to have the big house. All you have to do is say yes, and we can do this within a few months. I will have to put this cottage up for sale and give the proceeds to him. We will be gaining a far more valuable property and my new position with the Parramatta Livestock

Company means that we will have plenty of funds to keep a servant and also see to the grounds which have been neglected for so long.'

His wife had some good news of her own.

'Oh, Julian this couldn't have come at a better time. I am going to have a baby, so this larger house would be ideal, and I could certainly do with some extra help when that time arrives. The answer is yes.'

John kept his word, took the money from the sale of Julian's cottage, and returned to England. He did not maintain contact with the Australian branch of the family. Julian's family had grown: first a daughter, Emma and then twin boys, Jacob and Joshua. Living in a grand mansion was very pleasant. When Emma turned eighteen, she requested a garden party to celebrate. This meant a complete transformation of the old house, cleaning from top to bottom. During this time when everything was turned topsy-turvy, the linen cupboard came in for the same treatment. Emma watched as a servant climbed up on a little ladder to shift the contents of the top shelf. There were old pieces of bunting, calico and spare covers for the furniture, which had not been disturbed for a long time. An old calico bag aroused Emma's curiosity.

'Oh is that all this is, just an old spoon. We have got much better pieces in our canteen, although it has Papa's initials engraved on it. I had better show it to him.'

Off she flounced to the library and handed it to Julian who frowned at the sight of this object. Something stirred in the back of his mind, but he couldn't remember what it was.

'Thank you Emma. Leave it with me and I will sort it out later.'

As Emma left, Jacob entered the library. Noticing the spoon in his Father's hand he came closer to inspect it.

'What is that Papa? I haven't seen it in our silver canteen, and in actual fact it looks much older.'

'Yes Jacob, you are quite right. Emma brought it to me after one of the servants found it on the top shelf of our linen press. I can only guess that it belonged to your Uncle John. I doubt that he would be still alive, because he sailed for England before you were born. We have never heard from him since the day he left but I suppose that I really should inform him about this piece. It could have significance of some sort for him. I will write to his last address tonight.'

A reply arrived eventually, but it was not from John. His poor health prevented him from replying. However he managed to dictate an answer to his brother's enquiry. In essence, John knew little about the spoon. What he did recall was that their father, Lord Christie had once told him that he was putting something away for safe-keeping in the linen press and that it had been given to him by an old shipmate who had once served with him on the 'Endeavour'. Jacob was the only family member who showed any interest.

'Those initials that are engraved on it (J.C) are intriguing. They could have belonged to James Cook, or even my grandfather Jack Christie. If Uncle John didn't know any more about it, I guess we never will.'

Emma's eighteenth birthday was a huge success. She met her future husband who was introduced to her by Joshua. Before too long a wedding was planned for later that same year. Joshua moved to Sydney to further his career in the Bank. Only Jacob remained at home, caring for his Father after his Mother had passed away. He pursued his farming interests with the production of wheat and maize. As much as Jacob had little time for such things as silver spoons, he honoured his Father's wishes, explaining the story to his wife.

Because his Grandfather had sailed with Captain Cook, and this spoon had been on that voyage, it was to be considered a family heirloom. The spoon wasn't used or even admired by the family. Dormant in its calico bag, it was put into a dresser and forgotten. It continued to be passed down for another generation from Jacob to his son Joel, who was not interested at all in the legend or the spoon, but to please his Father he listened and committed the story to memory.

Joel's son Jamie was born in 1890 and by this time the family fortunes had become less impressive.

COOK'S SPOON

So much so that Joel was tempted to sell the dammed spoon, but because of the importance attached by previous relatives he handed it over to his son. Jamie packed it away, but in 1911 the dogs of war were barking and Jamie had other distractions.

— CHAPTER TWO —

A Silver Spoon is Found

T he will had been read, the old house had been sold, leaving just the contents to be sorted. Their mother was overseas so Myra and her sister Jill had offered to do this as it would give them closure after the death of their Nan. The kitchen was a real challenge as there were so many things to sort through which were broken, stained or just mismatched. These were hustled into boxes for the Salvo's. Myra sighed.

'Why ever did Nan keep all this old stuff? Surely she could have tossed it when it clearly was useless!'

Her sister pulled out the cutlery drawer. Little crumbs of stale food, rubber bands tie twisties and other droppings which did not bear thinking about, were all jumbled up in this drawer. Jill bundled them up and quickly put them into a plastic bag.

'Hold on a minute Jill,' said Myra as something caught her eye. 'There is an old drawstring bag at the back of the drawer. Let's have a look at it.'

Myra released the tie cord and peered inside. She gently eased out a silver serving spoon.

'Well look at this, Nan must have hidden this spoon for some reason. It seems to be in excellent condition.'

'Silver, nobody uses that stuff anymore. It always needs cleaning and the second hand shops are full of it. You can't give it away.'

'I'm going to keep this Jill, because it must have been important to her and I want to find out more about it.'

'Okay, suit yourself. The engraved initials aren't even hers or anyone else's in the family as far as I can tell. "J.C," the only J. C I know is Jesus Christ, and there is no way that this spoon ever belonged to Him.'

Turning the spoon over, Myra examined it more closely. It was quite heavy with a softly gleaming shaped bowl and a very long stem which was gracefully proportioned. She found the hallmarks which she knew would be there. There were some Latin words with a crest on the handle.

Jill had no use for silver. She was a modern Mum with a family that took up most of her time. Meals were plain and wholesome but if they had friends over it was a backyard barbecue with no frills. She had never owned any silver, had no desire to and could not see the value in buying such unnecessary and expensive items.

When they left the house, they were approached by the old lady from next door. Giving them her condolences, she noticed the bag in Myra's hand.

'What have you got there?' Marjorie asked.

'Oh, just an old silver spoon that we found in Nan's cutlery drawer,'said Myra.

'Yes I know the one. I often saw her clean and polish it, but she would never let me touch it. I asked her once where it came from and she told me 'Christies'. This did not make any sense to the two sisters but Myra made a mental note to take this up with her Mum when she arrived back from her holiday.

Vanessa was met by Myra at the airport, who chatted on about her overseas jaunt, and the fact that she had met someone wonderful.

'We have agreed to keep in touch. Since your father passed away I have been so lonely and after five years, it seems that I have at last found someone to share my life with.'

'But Mum, you have only been away for three months. How can you feel so strongly about someone that you hardly know?' Vanessa smirked with a knowing smile but did not elaborate.

A SILVER SPOON IS FOUND

'So how are things with you? Did you manage to sort out Nan's house and her belongings?'

'Yes Mum, Jill and I organized the sale and also the distribution of any saleable furniture, but there was one item that I wanted to talk to you about. In the cutlery drawer we found an old silver spoon. I don't recall ever seeing Nan use it.'

'So that's where it was. I looked high and low for that spoon some years ago. It is a long story but I will keep the details until after I have overcome jetlag and we can spend some more time together.'

'That's fine with me Mum, but my curiosity has been aroused and I think that a visit to a reputable silversmith might help with the identificationof the hallmarks.'

'Myra, can you wait for a day or two when we both can go together? There is a history attached to this spoon and it would be better if we both got our story straight before we take this any further.' With a stifled yawn, a perfunctory peck on her daughter's cheek, Vanessa said goodbye.

'Thanks darling for meeting my plane. I will phone you tomorrow. Please hold everything until then.'

As she drove away, Myra was bursting with unanswered questions, but she knew that her Mum would be tired. They could wait. Vanessa was tall and willowy with alabaster skin and thick auburn hair which Myra had inherited. She knew that her mother was a good looking woman, and therefore would still be attractive to men. She phoned Jill and told her the strange story that Mum had recounted about the spoon, and the fact that Mum had met some guy overseas.

Jill was not very interested. The kids had a cold, and she was feeling a little off herself, but she assured Myra that she would like to hear all about it later.

Two days passed. Vanessa asked her daughter to come over and to bring the spoon with her. After sitting down on the white leather lounge with mugs of steaming coffee, Vanessa began.

'This is a strange story, because such an incredible co-incidence has occurred in my life, that I hardly know whether to start at the end or the beginning. Perhaps if I tell you that David, my friend in England is a collector and an authority on Antique silver, it will help to explain the reason that I asked you to wait before going any further with your request.'

Myra felt the hair on the back of her neck rise. Why did Nan hide the silver spoon from her own daughter?

'Mum I accept that David is a legitimate authority, but why did Nan go to such pains to keep it hidden away? You have only just met David, whereas the search for it happened after Dad passed away some years ago.'

A SILVER SPOON IS FOUND

Vanessa took a long sip from her coffee mug, placed it on the glass and chrome table before she spoke.

'Before your Father died I met David in Australia at an Antiques Fair. He regularly comes here in search of interesting pieces, so I asked him about Mum's old spoon. He spoke about hallmarks, dropped shoulders, a tongue down the spoon's back and various things that I could not recall, let alone understand. I took his address and promised to contact him when I could. However with the event of your father's passing, I forgot all about the blessed spoon. When I got around to asking Nan about it, she became vague and could not remember where she had put it. David and I kept in touch, and when eventually I told him that my husband had died, he asked me to visit him in England. I didn't hesitate.'

Before Myra could say anything, the phone rang. Vanessa rose to answer it. Her face coloured as she spoke.

'When? When are you coming? Next Week? That is wonderful, just let me know your flight plans and I will meet you at the airport. Bye darling.'

She turned to her daughter. 'No prizes for guessing who that was. David is flying out here to attend another Antique Fair, so this would be an ideal time for him to give us an appraisal of that old spoon whilst he is here.'

'So soon, but you have only just said goodbye to him in England. Well perhaps he has a few reasons to come here. But why didn't you want me to take the spoon to a local silversmith?'

'You do have the right to know I suppose. Mum came by it from a rather questionable source. As a young woman she was a lady's maid to a married woman whose husband was serving overseas when our country was at war. This woman had an affair and became pregnant. She told Nan about it and was convinced that she had to abort the baby. Nan tried to dissuade her, but she was adamant, so Nan found a person to perform this task without risk to her employer. In those days there was little help with birth control but there were plenty of backyard butchers who would do the job. After this was successfully accomplished, Nan could do no wrong. She worked for this lady for many years where a strong bond was forged between them.

Their friendship continued long after Nan left her employment. She was given a generous payout and the silver spoon in appreciation. When I asked why she was given the spoon, she told me that it was the last reminder of an unhappy affair, as well as the man who had given it to her mistress.'

'Do I understand you correctly? This spoon which Nan has kept for years was given to her in appreciation for her help in procuring an abortion for her employer?

A SILVER SPOON IS FOUND

'Yes that is what she told me, but also one more thing. The man who gave it to her must have thought that he was coming back, because the spoon had his initials, "J.C." engraved on it. We will never know his identity. Nan seemed to think that there was something not kosher about the spoon's owner and because of her loyalty she kept it away from what she called, 'prying eyes.'

The week passed quickly and David's flight touched down at Mascot. Vanessa happily introduced him to her daughter. Myra's sister could not make it, because her youngest was teething and this had meant little sleep for the whole family. Dinner was an exciting affair because David had such a wonderful personality and kept them all in fits with his funny anecdotes. Myra could see why her Mum was so smitten by him.

After the main course, Vanessa served up home-made ice cream with fresh raspberries, then coffee and liqueurs rounded off a delicious dinner. David waited until the table had been cleared until he began to discuss the silver spoon which Vanessa had originally tried to identify. Myra handed it over, noting that his expression changed immediately. He held it, weighing it in one hand and then the other before giving it closer scrutiny. After turning the spoon over, he pulled out a jeweller's loupe and moved the spoon slowly back and forth until the hallmarks came into focus. Next he placed his forefinger gently on the marks and closed his eyes. When he opened them he was smiling.

'I think I will first give you a crash course on how to date and understand what the hallmarks tell you. These hallmarks can differ in sequence, sometimes left to right, sometimes not. Sometimes the maker's initials are at the beginning, sometimes at the end. Hallmarks can be horizontal or vertical.

If we read from the left to the right, it is usually the case that the Silver Standard comes first, indicating the purity which can be produced in England, Scotland or Ireland. Next is the city mark, which can be London, Birmingham, Chester, Exeter, Newcastle, Sheffield etc. The third mark is the Date letter which is a bit tricky to explain because the date letter system was used to test the silver content when a piece was presented for assay or testing. These marks were changed annually and each cycle differed by changing the font, letter case and shield shapes. We can forget about this for the time being. The fourth mark is the Duty mark which was so called because in 1784 a tax was imposed to pay duty to the crown.

This mark used was a profile portrait of the reigning monarch's head. The last and fifth mark belonged to the maker. Its purpose was to prevent forgery of the leopard's head by indicating the party responsible for the piece.'

A SILVER SPOON IS FOUND

Vanessa and Myra's heads were spinning with all these details.

'Now comes the interesting part, we can read this spoon fairly easily because it has provided us with all we need to know. Reading from the left we find the maker's initials first which are: 'E.J.', next we can just see the Lion Passant Guardant which indicates Sterling Silver. The date letter is 'O' which indicates the year 1750. There is no duty mark which was created in 1784, so this spoon was made before that date. It is not crucial to date our spoon exactly because we have information from the hallmarks that I have mentioned, including the maker.'

'Why is he so important?' asked Vanessa.

'For a start he was a she. Elizabeth Jackson - Oldfield was a well respected silversmith, and unless I miss my educated guess, this old spoon has rarity, is in very good condition and could prove to be quite valuable.'

Vanessa was silent for a second or two before looking at Myra.

'Well Myra, what do you think about Nan's secret now? She probably wouldn't have had any idea of its worth or even where it came from.'

Myra nodded, deciding to give her Mum and David some privacy, so she gave her thanks and said goodnight.

What David had failed to mention was the fact that the Latin inscription on the handle which said

"Circa orbem" (around the world), as well as the initials "J.C.", indicated that this spoon had provenance of great interest. He had a sneaking suspicion about the spoon's first owner, but Myra needed convincing to follow this up.

Vanessa had noticed the engraved crest and initials and even with her limited knowledge of silver hallmarks, she knew that all of these clues could be the key to authenticating the spoon. She also knew her daughter very well. It was up to her to follow her own path of discovery.

The Silver spoon had celebrated two hundred years of birthdays, but Myra knew that she wanted to get some answers before the next two hundred, so she decided to visit the only person who could shed some light on the matter, Nan's neighbour, Marjorie.

When she arrived, Marjorie was in the front garden watering her plants. She gave Myra a shy smile before saying.

'I knew that I would see you again love, it's about the spoon isn't it? You had better come in, I am due for a cuppa and we can have a nice chat. You came without your sister. Is she well?'

Nodding to Marjorie, Myra took a chair at the small table.

'I asked you about your sister, because your Nan told me that Jill was never really interested in what Betty had in that drawer. Over the years I got to know your Nan pretty well. I know that she was a little disappointed when Jill told her that all that sort of stuff belonged in a second hand shop or worse. When I saw that you had found it I didn't say any more because I had to wait for you to come to me.'

'What are you talking about Marjorie, is there something else that I should know?'

'There is much more to the story, because Betty left her diary with me and also her instructions that I should give it to no-one except you. Before I hand it over, I will ask you to promise not to reveal the contents to anyone else.'

Myra agreed then watched Marjorie waddle down the hallway. In a minute she returned with a thick old brown leather book tied together with string.

As she handed it over she said.

'Lots of things change over the years, but true love never does.'

'Thank you for this Marjorie. Perhaps it will explain something about the spoon that seemed to be so important to my grandmother. Goodbye.'

With controlled impatience Myra drove home, poured a cup of tea, kicked off her shoes, took the phone off the hook and lay down on the lounge. For hours she stayed glued to the diary. It grew dark outside but apart from switching on a standard lamp, her eyes saw nothing else except the words on the page. After a while the tears slowly formed as she felt a real sympathy for someone that she never knew. At times she shook her head in disbelief. She thought to herself.

'How strange that Nan's story has affected me in a way that the silver spoon's possible origin and value never could. She kept it all those years in memory of a dear friend, as a symbol of a sad loss and a wasted life.'

— CHAPTER THREE —

The Spoon of Sorrow

Australia 1952

Myra read every page, but then returned to the diary and followed certain passages that she felt were the essential part of this narrative.

"Today I have found employment with the sweetest young woman that I could ever hope to meet. Her name is Laura, and I am to call her by that name. She and her husband live in a modest home, but as she is so frail and mostly confined to her bed, it is necessary to employ help.

Sometimes she is happy and we share a common love of the garden as well as the outdoor enjoyment of the birds that seem to want to cheer her up.

I have found her in bed again, but she has covered her face with a piece of fabric, and I am concerned about her. When she rang her little gold bell I entered her bedroom with a weak cup of tea and almost dropped the tray. Her lovely face was swollen and there were dark bruises evident on her face and forearms. She was quick to tell me that she had fallen out of bed and this was 'her fault.'

Not wanting to be seen to be judgmental about her husband, but he does not appear to have any concern about her condition and there are few words exchanged between them in my presence. She tries to be civil and uncomplaining to him, but he only exacerbates this weakness and is harshly critical of her even in front of me.

This week I have discussed her state with her husband because her melancholy seems to be increasing, and her little face is swollen constantly where she has been crying. No amount of powder can camouflage that. He is not interested and even worse has threatened me with dismissal if I continue to complain about his wife's 'weakness.'

To be cheerful is my nature, but her silence and disinterest in most things about her really challenges my personality. Today I had to physically help her outside, as her legs seemed ill-fit to carry her. The winter sun warmed us both, and she managed to throw a few crumbs of bread to the cheerful and busy birds. It wasn't too long before she tired of this and wanted to rest again. By now I had noticed a little weight loss and became alarmed at her condition. Tactfully I enquired if she had seen a doctor lately, to which the tears again formed in her eyes. She informed me that her husband thought that she was faking ill health just for his sympathy.

I must not interfere between husband and wife, but this situation is developing into a serious crisis. What can I do? She gave me a key to let myself into the house, as I often arrived after her husband had left for work, and as usual it was a silent and cold greeting. After making the tea and toast for her, I knocked on her door and entered the bedroom.

There she was lying on the floor, but this time her nightdress was torn and I could see blood oozing from cuts to her face and body.

Laura, what has happened? I knelt onto the floor next to her where my emotions could not be checked. I cried for this poor little lady who did not deserve this. I could see his bloodied belt and buckle lying in the corner of the room where he had thrown it after beating her. She was moaning which was really a good sign as I had feared that she might be dead.

This time I did not hesitate to call the doctor. Dear battered Laura was taken to hospital where I spent many hours with tears beneath the surface. She would not admit that her husband had performed this evil act, but she told me the truth in private. She begged me not to reveal it and because of her weakened state, I concurred.

He did not come to visit her, which was just as well, because if I had seen him, I could not be sure of my self-control.

She was allowed home after a week and strangely he was nowhere to be found. He had left her a letter which explained that he was sick of a complaining and useless wife and that he was going to enlist in the army to enjoy the company of healthy and happy men. No apologies were given.

Laura blamed herself for his decision, and no amount of my argument changed her mind about this. I continued to do her bidding and after a while the colour returned to her cheeks and her lovely eyes took on a more alert expression. She put on a little weight and seemed to enjoy her outings both in the garden and shopping down the street. She informed me that she would only require my services once a week, as her finances and her return to health dictated this new plan. I agreed to this but told her that I would come and visit her as a friend on odd occasions if she so wished. She smiled at this suggestion and agreed that it could benefit us both.

Quite a few months passed and I noticed a big change in her. She seemed to be happy almost all of the time. Her cheeks were flushed and she often hummed little tunes to herself in the garden where she now spent a lot of time pruning the roses, weeding the flower beds and chatting to the numerous birds who knew where and when to visit.

She never actually told me how they met, but she had a 'friend,' and to me this was the best news that I could possibly hope for. His name was Jamie Christie and he was a little younger than her, but he made her laugh: the results of which were very evident in this lonely lady.

One day when I was visiting her she seemed a little quiet and I felt that our friendship was strong enough for me to enquire about this. We were sitting outside in the sun sipping a cold glass of home-made lemonade. The soft breeze was blowing her blonde curls around her shoulders, and she was a picture of good health. She hesitated for a moment before answering me.

"Betty, what I have to tell you is for your ears only. I can hardly believe my own happiness. I have fallen in love with a wonderful young man and the feeling is so foreign to me that I tremble every time that I think about him. His touch is gentle, his love is earnest and his heart is mine. We have become so close that I fear for my chastity, but I dare not tell him that I am married."

Now I understood. Her evident happiness had made such a wonderful change in her, so I told her. Laura you are married in one sense only; a piece of paper. It is said that the laws of nature are stronger than the laws of man.

When I left that afternoon, I thought that she was at peace, but I also felt a sense of guilt because I had condoned what was really an adulterous relationship. How could I not wish her a little happiness after what she had suffered at the hands of that monster? She did not need my approval but she had it anyway.

My visit today found her crying tears of joy. She was pregnant. For years she had cherished a secret hope that this would one day happen to her, but her husband blamed her and abused her pervertedly when they tried to conceive. She wanted to tell Jamie, but as it was early days yet she was going to wait for a while. Making my usual weekly visit to her, I entered the house and sensed that something was wrong. Laura would always be waiting for me with a cuppa and a happy greeting. Not so today. In her bedroom I found her curled up fully dressed on top of her quilt. Her face told me that she had been crying and that this was not from happiness. She let out a howl when she first saw me and then began to sob uncontrollably.

I couldn't believe that this was the same woman that I had seen last week. Sitting beside her I listened to her disjointed story which was sometimes unintelligible because of the emotion that swept over her. Jamie had come to see her last night and was particularly affectionate telling her that he loved her deeply. She was his night and day and he would treasure the time spent together. Would she promise to wait until he returned to marry her?

With this another deep wracking tremor overtook Laura. I realized without having to ask that she had not told him about the baby. She continued 'return, return from where?' Jamie informed her that he had enlisted in the army as the war was imminent and he wanted to make this country a safer place for when he returned to Laura.

It was so hard for me to say anything at this stage, but I promised to look after her as I had always done. I was about to go into the kitchen to put on the kettle when Laura called me back. She wanted to show me something that Jamie had given to her. Between sobs she explained.

"As he had no time or money to buy an engagement ring, he gave me the only thing of value that he possessed. It is lying on the table in a white fabric bag."

I picked it up and opened it. What a surprise I got. It contained an old silver serving spoon with the initials 'J.C.' engraved on the handle. It could not have been Jamie's spoon because it was obviously an antique. I returned it with a sinking feeling. What was to become of this poor little lamb whose only sin in life was to love a man with her whole being?

War is abhorrent, life is unfair and fate can be predetermined.

Laura's husband died in the same war that took Jamie's life but worse still to relate, she wanted to terminate the life that was growing inside her. She loved Jamie so much but the fact that he was going to war was more than she could bear and she didn't want to face the future without him. His child was not an option for her.

Myra knew the rest of the story because her Mother had told her that Nan had helped Laura end the unwanted pregnancy which must have affected her deeply. She would have tried everything to prevent this, but only a threat from Laura to end her own life would have over-ridden this awful dilemma. She already knew that it had an unhappy ending and she also knew why Nan had the old silver spoon in her kitchen drawer. The diary had left her with a strong resolution regarding the spoon, but her Mother had to be convinced that it should not be sold.

Vanessa was more than happy to discuss the spoon and invited her daughter to come over. When she arrived, they were both sipping cocktails and invited Myra to join them. She came straight to the point.

'I have been giving the spoon a lot of thought and have decided that I want it to remain as it has for possible centuries: at rest and in my keeping.'

'But it has no sentiment attached to it as far as I am concerned and as Nan didn't seem to display or use it I can't see why you would want it under these conditions,' her Mother replied.

Although David did not want to enter into this discourse, he felt that he should give Myra a chance at perhaps changing her mind.

THE SPOON OF SORROW

'Myra after all the presentation of the dated facts about the possible provenance of this spoon, it could be a valuable piece. It would have been produced in the reign of George the Second. It is well known that during the Georgian period, the art of the silversmith achieved real greatness with beauty of design and excellence of execution. The other point of interest is that even though we take silver for granted today, this spoon would have belonged to someone of high rank in the community. The gentry or nobility were the only ones who could afford such luxuries and if any records exist of the spoon's sale, the consequences could have great import. Having a family crest and motto would be easy to research if you feel so inclined.'

Myra knew that David believed that what he said would tip the scales in his opinion, but he didn't know just what her Nan thought about the spoon and how much it meant to her. So no, she was immovable in her decision.

'Thank you David for all your help and wonderful expertise about the whole situation but I have decided not to sell it or take it any further for authentication. Please understand that my Nan kept it for a reason. She probably could have sold it if she had wanted to but she chose to keep it in accordance to her principles. I can do no less.'

Vanessa looked at David who shook his head. She knew that once her daughter had made up her mind there would be no changing it. A few days later Vanessa rang Myra telling her that David was flying back to the U.K. on business but he hoped to visit Australia again in the near future

Myra was pleased for her Mother's sake as she felt that they both had a genuine interest in each other. Taking the spoon out of its calico bag she ran her fingers over the engraving and said out aloud.

'Oh Jamie, if only you knew how much she loved you. It doesn't seem as if this spoon has ever brought happiness to anyone.'

Myra knew that this spoon must remain packed away again until she felt that the time was right to unlock its secret origin. Returning it to its calico bag, she placed it in the back of a drawer in her dressing table.

— CHAPTER FOUR —

The Queen's Spoon

England 1952

Archie and Stan slowly shuffled past the wonderful treasures that were on display in the Tower of London. The Crown Jewels were something to see. Archie was enthralled with the Coronation or Anointing Spoon, but because he could not read very well he asked the guard about their history.

'This Coronation Spoon has been used in coronations of British Monarchs since the 12th and early 13th century. It is the only remaining piece of the original Royal Regalia because Charles the First disposed of some of the other items and the remainder was melted down.'

'Cor, gov, it must be real valuable,' said Archie. 'As anyone tried to nick off with it?'

The guard sniffed, looked down his nose at the source of this question and after raising his head and staring straight ahead, continued.

'Yes in 1301 a robbery did take place in the ancient Treasury of Westminster Abbey. The Abbot of Westminster and forty eight brethren and thirty two other persons were indicted for the robbery. Of course they all claimed that they were falsely charged.

'Blimey,' said Stan, 'did they get frown in the clink?'

The Beefeater smiled as he recalled the scheme which had provided these men with such a haul.

'The perpetrator was so bold in his undertaking that he used a ladder to enter the Chapter House through an upstairs window with such success that he could not carry all the loot. What he couldn't handle he put into leather pouches and covered them with the soil behind the Church to retrieve them later. He was caught red-handed but he soon revealed the details of how he managed so easily to rob the place with a lot of help from others. Of course he and his accomplices were all given sentences.

When James the Second came to the throne he found that so many of the precious stones from the Crown of England had been stolen and replaced with imitations that he had to make good these jewels to the tune of twelve thousand pounds. Because of this debacle the Crown Jewels were moved to their new home which is where you see them today.'

THE QUEEN'S SPOON

'Ta gov,' said Archie as he tipped his hat and shoved Stan along the passageway. He turned and whispered.

'Did ya see that silva spoon?'

'Wot silva spoon?'

'The one we first seed when we came in 'ere.'

Stan did not recall it and said with a grin.

'I fought the dish ran away wif the spoon.'

'Wat in hell are you babbling on about?'

'You noe, the dish ran away wif the spoon becuz the knife had already gotten the fork outta there.'

Archie frowned and then hit Stan on the top of his head with his bunched fist.

'Don't you lissen to nothing? That geyser told us abart dem jules and ow they were replaced wif imitations. Doesn't it ring a bell?'

Stan looked mystified but Archie's head was buzzing with ideas about that Silver Gilt Spoon. For a couple of days Archie and Stan made a few visits to the Tower and the Crown Jewels. These excursions were made when there was a different guard on duty so as not to raise any suspicions.

'Blimey I'm sure that there are 'idden alarms everywhere becuz the glass looks to be six inches fick. This carn't be easy Stan.'

Stan had no ideas about such things and he just blinked at Archie.

'Eh, Archie I seen a spoon just like that one in a pawn shop in Portobello Road,' whispered Stan.

'You steaming great git. That's the only one in existence.'

'Orright then let's go there 'n you take a peek.' a subdued Stan replied.

Archie went home and put on his cleanest dirty shirt with the crumpled cravat at his neck before he took off for the pawn shop. He could not believe his eyes because sure enough there was a silver gilt spoon identical to the one that lay in all its glory in the Tower, sitting there in the window. The price tag was one hundred pounds.

Archie slid over to the counter and asked to see that 'ole spoon' in the window. When it was presented to him he turned it over and was dismayed to see that it didn't have any hallmarks.

'This is only a replica' Archie was told, 'and that is why the price is so reasonable.' Archie was more than happy to hand over a ten pound note as a deposit and declared that he would return with the balance.

'That was a great 'fing what you done Stan. Now I'm gonna see my 'ole man who is a right villen and always has come cash kickin abart. My plan is to buy this ere reptile so that I can swop it wif the real one.'

Archie's Dad listened to the scam and showed great interest as all robberies and such pursuits were his bread and butter.

The details were just as interesting because Archie planned to use his Dad as a Yeoman Warder.

His age was right and dressed in that colourful costume, he would look like all the rest of them.

'Right then, when does all this 'appen? Ave you got a date son?'

'Yea Dad, the jools will be taken out soon to be cleaned for the Coronation an that is when we swop the spoons.'

'Just one thing Arch, I wants to see the spoon at the pawn shop because I knows old Ikey the owner and I want to check it out.'

When they fronted up to the shop, Ikey said.

'Hello Merv, what brings you here?'

'You and me goes back a long way and I 'ave put some good bizness your way, if you gets my meaning, so just to be sure that you are on the up and up I want you to discount this spoon for my boy who is really skint. Perhaps a fifty per cent deduction would be fair eh? After all it's only a replica aint it?'

Ikey had been a known fence for years, so he agreed to Merv's idea. The balance of forty pounds was handed over to Ikey. He gave the spoon with a receipt for a value of fifty pounds to Archie. This was done on a fresh pawn ticket in case the spoon was to be returned for cash.

They had to be patient. The three villains took turns in watching the movements in and out of the Tower. The date for the Coronation had already been set. The Royal Jewellers, Garrard and Company would be doing the maintenance and cleaning. The window of opportunity was very limited for this exchange to be done successfully with crucial timing needed.

Arch had located the Guards' clothesline and managed to steal a uniform from it. With the letters 'E.R.' emblazoned across the front, this was the blue 'undress uniform' which was used by the Tower Guards on duty. Merv was dressed ready to play his part with the replica spoon hidden in his uniform between the elbow and wrist. All he had to do was to exchange the spoons at the precise time when it was being removed from the glass case. Archie and Stan disguised as Ambulance drivers would create a diversion. Everything went as planned. Archie and Stan 'borrowed' an ambulance and drove it into the courtyard with sirens screaming five minutes after the Garrard's van arrived. Merv was now bent over doubled as he shuffled towards the other guards that were removing the Crown Jewels from the display cabinet. He was clutching at his heart and moaning. As he leant against the far wall, Archie and Stan came rushing in asking for the Senior Yeoman who had called the ambulance. The guards immediately became suspicious and called for reinforcements, just as Merv stumbled against the open cabinet switching the two spoons. As soon as his was done, he fell to the floor simulating a heart attack.

'Right' said Archie. 'This ere gent needs some proper attention real fast.'

THE QUEEN'S SPOON

They wasted no time in picking Merv up from the floor, transporting him to the ambulance whilst the astonished guards looked on. A quick inspection of the cabinet showed that all looked in order, so there was no reason to be alarmed. The guards found that nothing was missing so they put it down to a strange mix-up. Little did they know how much of a mix-up.

The ambulance was left in a deserted area where they all changed back into their normal clothes. Merv had wrapped the spoon in an old white handkerchief, quickly shoving it into his pocket. The trio walked home to Merv's lodgings and sat down at the kitchen table to examine their precious cargo.

With trembling fingers Archie couldn't open it quickly enough to stare at his prize. He had seen pictures in the papers of the Crown Jewels but the Coronation Spoon had completely captured his heart.

(This spoon is decorated with four freshwater pearls set in the widest part of the handle with a design which predates Christianity. A thin bowl joins the stem by a modified elbow depicting a leopard with a central ridge which contains anointing oil used to anoint the Monarch. The concave side of the bowl is beautifully patterned with swirls of arabesque intricate designs).

Archie and Merv were still drooling over this magnificent object, when a loud banging on the front door shocked them.

'Ere Dad, ave we been snookered already? Oo would be that be knocking? Quick 'ide the spoon in the drawer,' hissed Archie.

After Merv did this he slowly ambled to the door which was being pounded so strongly that the glass panels were threatening to disintegrate at any moment. He could see the outline of the other person standing on the other side, recognized him and opened the door.

'Watch'er Ikey, no need to bust me bleedin door down. What's up?

Ikey rushed in mopping his hatchet face with a hanky. His eyes were bloodshot and his clothes looked as if he slept in them.

'Merv, where is that spoon that I sold you? Have you still got it? Tell me that you haven't done anything silly with it?'

'What are you going on about? We paid you good money for that spoon. Why are you asking?

Ikey pulled out a chair, flopped into it and began to tell his tale of woe.

'I don't know how to tell you this, but I think that the replica that I sold you was in fact the original.'

Archie sat bolt upright at this terrible news. An electric current had just run up his spine.

'Wot? Ow can you know this? It didn't ave any fancy marks on it and you musta got it from a dodgy customer, who would have sold it as a repulca,' Archie growled.

'Yes I did buy it as a replica because there have been many copies circulating for some time of varying accuracy and quality. When he read about the Coronation, the bloke that originally sold it to me rang from overseas to ask if I still had it. He is keen to buy it back from you because after he did some research he found that the original spoon was rebuilt and regilt for the 1661 Coronation. It is decorated with an Arabesque pattern, but this bloody spoon, the most valuable English spoon in existence does not possess and 'authenticating marks.'

'Ikey are you telling us that the spoon that you sold to us for fifty nicker is actually worth millions?'

Ikey nodded his head as the tears began to fil his eyes.

'This is a catastrophe for me, but it you have it we can still benefit from the sale.'

Merv spoke up. 'A word Arch in the next room.'

Seriously concerned about what his son might say or do, now that Ikey had told them about their purchase, Merv did some quick thinking.

'The one that we bought as a replica is now in the Tower and it possibly is the priceless original, but although we can't return the spoon in the drawer to the Tower, it still could have some value for sale. Leave this up to me.'

Merv cleared his throat and said to Ikey.

'Ikey, this is a dicey situation. We all go back a long way, so me and Arch are prepared to do a deal, but first I ave to get some advice like.'

Ikey agreed, shook hands and departed.

Merv found Stan asleep on the lounge, so he shook him till he was awake.

'Stan, you have a reel important job to do. Go to the local paper shop and buy a magnifying glass so that we can examine this spoon. Mum's the word if you get my meaning.'

In a short time Stan arrived back with the magnifying glass. Archie looked lovingly at the spoon first with ooh's and aah's as he closely examined it. After a few minutes he handed them both to his Dad. Merv carried out a painstakingly slow inspection. A frown began to deepen his brow. This spoon didn't have any hallmarks either. What did this mean? Was it possibly another replica? This was very confusing and it needed to be cleared up very quickly.

'Wot do ya fink abart this Dad? Ow come this one doesn't ave any hallmarks either?

'There 'as been many robberies in the Tower. Maybe the original Anointing Spoon was lifted and replaced with a replica that passed muster over the years.'

Neither the spoon in their possession nor the one bought from Ikey had any hallmarks. It would take an expert to define any other distinguishing marks so Merv felt that they could still have a good result.

THE QUEEN'S SPOON

'In answer to your question son, I'm sure that we can sell this ere spoon and still have a nice little earner. I'm off to ave a chat with a friend of mine who is very cluey about this kind of fing. Just wrap the spoon up in a hanky and hide it I the bottom of the laundry basket.'

Merv took a bus to Soho where he found his chum Peter. After turning the sign around to say 'closed,' Peter locked the shop's door behind them. No small talk was needed because Peter knew just what would bring Merv to see him and it wasn't to discuss each other's health.

Peter indicated a chair to Merv, while he took up a seat opposite at his desk.

'What are you up to my friend?' he asked.

'I've found myself in a bit of a dodgy situation you might say an' I need some advice from you about a delicate matter.'

Peter raised an eyebrow. This was a different approach. Usually Merv wanted something valued, but this sounded like a more personal problem.

'Go ahead Merv, I'm all ears.'

'Well it's like this see, I know a certain cove what has in his hands a replica of a coronation spoon that came from the Tower of London. This was exchanged for another replica that was placed in the cabinet there.'

Merv continued to tell Peter the details about the pawn shop sale where they bought a replica which could in fact be the real thing. Peter asked him how he knew that one was genuine and that one was not.

'The pawn shop owner told us that the original spoon doesn't 'ave any hallmarks to authenticate it, but the bloke wat sold it to him wants to buy it back at any price. I don't know if one is the original or if they are both fakes.'

'My friend, I have to tell you this and I'm afraid that it will not help you at all but Replica Coronation spoons have been around for hundreds of years. This all began about 1885 and they would have been made every year except during the two world wars. It would be impossible to authenticate both these spoons if they are not hallmarked. The only thing that I can suggest is that you bring them both to me and I will give you my best opinion about them.'

'Er, well I 'aven't got them both anymore, I only 'ave one. It came from the Tower and the one that came from the pawn shop is back in the Tower.'

Peter let out a loud laugh which was not what Merv wanted to hear. This was a terrible problem and he needed some help before he made his next move.

'It sounds as if you have got the tiger by the tail. You can't return the spoon taken from the Tower without a whole lot of explaining and the one that is supposedly authentic is back where it should have been in the first place.'

THE QUEEN'S SPOON

'Yea well what I wants to know is can we sell the one that we took from the Tower to a client at the pawnshop. Would it be good enough to fool im?'

'If the one from the Tower was good enough to fool the authorities who have cleaned and handled it all these years it would be good enough to sell to the pawnshop's client. But be careful, if you ask for millions you will never get it. By the same token if you sell it too cheap someone will smell a rat. My advice to you is that you let them make an offer, then negotiate. Good luck.'

Merv thanked Peter for his help hoping that Ikey's client would be willing to pay a good deal to own the spoon even if it was only a 'replica.' Archie was agreeable with his Dad's plan. When Ikey was told about the 'spoon' now being for sale, he seemed to be relieved. He informed Merv that his client was overseas but was interested in arranging a meeting when he returned.

What he didn't tell Ikey was that the spoon in his keeping was not the same spoon that Archie had bought from the pawnshop. In fact it was from the Tower of London!

— CHAPTER FIVE —

Sold

England 1953

Ikey was excited. He knew that Archie and Merv were just as keen as his special client to have this meeting. The four men met in Ikey's office where the spoon was handed over for inspection. A loupe was produced and a great deal of time was spent in examination of the spoon. As agreed they waited for the buyer to do the talking. The man with the poker face said.

'I am not sure what you are trying to pull, but this is not the same spoon that I sold to Ikey. It is a replica and a very good one at that, but it is not what I came here to buy.'

This was not what they expected to hear.

'You had better tell me the whole story and we will take it from there.'

'Before I do that,' said Merv, 'How much is this one worth?'

David took his time and let the silence deepen before he spoke.

'Probably about one thousand pounds, you all know that it has no hallmarks to authenticate it so it could pass as a possible original to someone gullible enough to buy it.'

Merv scratched his chin, cleared his throat and decided to tell the truth about the Coronation Spoon.

'Your spoon that we bought from Ikey now rests in the Tower of London. We swopt it for this one, thinkin that we had the original. Now we finds out that this is a replica too. If this one is such a good one as you say, why don't you give us the money an you can keep it.'

David played it cool.

'You have been up to no good haven't you? I am really so terribly disappointed about the loss of my spoon but I am not likely to retrieve it now from the Tower. Being a sensible businessman I can probably manage to sell your replica to my advantage. If we do a deal and it is a distinct possibility, I will phone Ikey and he will contact you.'

Archie didn't really trust this man but as they had little option, he went along with his Dad's counsel. The very next morning Ikey who sounded as if his feelings had been severely hurt, rang.

'Okay you can bring the spoon here. He has agreed to buy it.'

Arch and Merv handed over the spoon as David handed over one thousand pounds in cash. Hands were shaken and everyone left feeling happy.

One thousand pounds was a lot of money, and after giving Stan a sling of fifty pounds, Arch and his Dad split the rest.

David had to cut short his trip to Australia because he had been informed about an upcoming auction which was offering some interesting pieces, including a set of six spoons made in 1936 for the coronation of Edward V111 which never took place.

The replica of the coronation spoon sold to Ikey, which had been purchased from a dubious source was something that he wanted to offload quickly without any questions being asked. When he thought that he could re-sell it because of all the interest in the upcoming Coronation, David had hoped to buy it back.

What happened here today was beyond his wildest dreams.

The 'replica' which had been swapped from the Tower was in fact the original. It took a trained eye to search for the markings which were not hallmarked as all other valuable pieces are. The bowl of the Anointing Spoon was so beautifully decorated and scrolled that the pattern his its most important detail. When the spoon was re-gilded in 1661, it was marked with the silversmith's initials cleverly hidden amongst the swirling patterns. They were almost invisible to the naked eye, but between two floral emblems in the shape of an ancient 'fleur-de-lis' David found the authentication that he was looking for.

He had been collecting anointing replicas for years and had no less than two hundred of them in differing sizes. Some were bought overseas from Holland and Canada, but all were beautiful. Tonight his veneration was sublime.

David took the Anointing Coronation Spoon to his glass cabinet and gently laid his new acquisition in a place which he had carefully prepared. He locked it, slid the painting across the cavity, poured himself a brandy and retired to bed.

Captain Cook's voyage referenced from 'The Picturesque Atlas of Australasia' 1886

PART TWO

— CHAPTER ONE —

The Collector

England 1953

David was a contented man. He had everything in life to make him happy. Well almost. Within his London Mayfair flat he kept a secret which he could not share with anyone. To own a piece of the Crown Jewels was possibly a treasonable offence. His passion for silverware had also been his lifelong obsession. There were many who shared this with him but not all were as successful. David personally knew of some who had managed to 'acquire' paintings which had disappeared from Art galleries and private collections. He had been blessed with incredible luck managing to acquire the crowning piece in his collection of replica 'anointing spoons.' His latest acquisition was not a replica. Through the ignorance of the men selling it and by his own guile in playing it cool he now owned the priceless Coronation Anointing Spoon.

Many years ago his wife died, and although David had a son in South Africa they rarely contacted each other. Colleagues with similar interests were always within reach, but now he had little incentive to improve his collection. He did have one other strong interest in his life: her name was Vanessa.

Some years ago they met in Australia and the memory of her loveliness still stirred him. They both found similar interests at an Antiques Fair where they hit it off straight away. She was honest and without any pretensions, and David felt that they had reconnected in Australia recently. Perhaps it was time to see if she felt the same about him. Australia beckoned, so he rang Vanessa and told her that he was coming over and had a very important question to ask her.

CHAPTER TWO

Romancing the Spoon

Australia 1953

Vanessa stood before the open French doors that led out to a small balcony. She wore a long white satin nightdress with small shoestring straps. Feeling the soft night breeze wash over her through the transparent curtains, her body felt warm, but it was not because of the summer evening temperature. She was a mature woman who felt that perhaps she could dare to hope for a life which still held some unfulfilled dreams. Vanessa had to admit that she was a little excited about tomorrow.

Placing her hands on her flat stomach she knew that her breasts were not generous but David had made her feel completely happy about herself. He seemed to admire her for exactly who she was. After losing her husband some years ago, Vanessa was discreet about her relationship with David, but time was marching on and her loneliness grew with every passing year. She went early to the airport and found him immediately. A tall handsome man whose hair was turning grey at the temples, with a frame that seemed to suggest a military background, he strode purposely towards her. Dropping his briefcase, he took her into his arms.

'Oh, David, I have missed you so much. When you flew back to England, I had no idea of when I would see you again.'

He chuckled, gave her a quick kiss and said. 'Forget about that. I am here now, and we have some important things to discuss.'

When they arrived back at the house David half lay on the lounge, and relaxed after his long flight.

'Let me look at you,' he said. 'Vanessa you grow more beautiful every time that I see you. Could I ask you for a cup of tea?'

Vanessa went to the kitchen to prepare a pot of tea but when she returned David was sound asleep. She smiled as she draped a quilt over his sleeping form.

'Sleep well, my darling,' she whispered before she climbed the stairs to her bedroom. Just before dawn she felt something tickling her nose. Opening her eyes, she saw David standing in the background, a silhouette against the transparent curtains which gently swayed behind him. In his hands was a breakfast tray with a lovely fresh rose from the garden and a glass of orange juice. Her hunger for food was not aroused yet, and David had deliberately not included food anyway. He slipped into bed beside her warm and soft body.

'Please forgive my bad manners last night. I didn't mean to fall asleep, but I was so tired. We have so much to talk about, but first I want to make love to you.' Vanessa smiled, opening her arms with an unmistakable invitation. Making love made her feel alive in a way which she had almost forgotten. Later she arose, showered and went down to the kitchen singing. 'Some enchanted evening.' This euphoric state continued as she rustled up Eggs Benedict, toast and marmalade and a pot of coffee. When David joined her at the table, he took her hands in his.

'Vanessa, will you marry me?'

Without hesitation she said, 'yes David, I will.'

A dinner party was arranged for the whole family to hear the news. Jill and her husband Brian seemed pleased for Vanessa. Myra was quietly thrilled. David announced that their wedding would be in London, and that he was prepared to pay the airfares for all the family. To Myra he dangled a little extra carrot.

'This would be a great opportunity for you to bring that spoon over and do some research. You never know what you may unearth.'

'Thank you David, but as time will be limited, I shall keep myself otherwise occupied.' Myra grinned at him. She needed little urging as this would be a trip of a lifetime and her mother's happiness was infectious. Jill thanked David assuring him that they would think about it and let him know.

'Don't take too long,' he joked. 'We are not getting any younger and we have a lot of living to do.'

Jill and her husband decided that the trip would be too much for the whole family, as their youngest was only two years old. They thanked David for his generous offer and wished the couple a long and happy marriage. Within a month David and Vanessa had left Australia for London. Myra managed to conclude her commitments, and was invited to stay in David's flat. He was happy to be home for many reasons. Not least of which was to be reunited with the magnificent treasure that he kept under his roof. Hoping that Vanessa would share his joy with this acquisition, he decided that it wasn't the right time to tell her about it just yet.

David had managed to contact his son John in South Africa, and he had agreed to attend the wedding which took place on a lovely spring day.

— CHAPTER THREE —

Myra and John Learn a Little about Spoons

England 1953

One of David's colleagues had offered his home for the wedding reception. Myra was amazed at the beautiful Regency period décor: the striped silk wallpaper, the heavy gold framed paintings and the incredible furniture. What was really outstanding was the beautiful bathroom with its lovely blue and white floral patterned toilet bowl and cistern. There was also a porcelain pull handle with the same design. As Myra closed the bathroom door behind her and stepped back, she collided with David's son John, who always seemed polite but aloof. He was also staying at his father's apartment, and preferred to have his nose in a book, rather than make conversation.

'Oops, sorry,' she said as she stepped on his foot. 'I think that this upstairs bathroom has the most amazing antique suite that I have ever laid eyes on.' John did not look faintly interested but as she had made this remark he had to say something.

'I am sorry Myra, but I do not feel that an investigation into the quality of a bathroom's fittings is warranted at a wedding reception. Do you?'

Her eyes flared with anger, she turned on her new black patent high heels and deliberately stuck her heel into his shoe. As she tossed her head at him she said.

'I'm sorry too.'

She thought. 'Not only is he boring but he is an incredible snob.'

Myra knew that both she and John had been asked to remain in David's flat until after the newlyweds had returned from a short honeymoon in Paris, so it was impossible to avoid some conversation, so polite John became even more uninteresting in Myra's eyes. At breakfast she was always late, which did not seem to worry him at all, but at night she would go into the kitchen whilst he was reading his news-paper in the drawing room, cook a meal for two and then consume hers before he could join her. This all came to a head when John had

MYRA AND JOHN
LEARN A LITTLE ABOUT SPOONS

had enough of her attitude and decided to do something about it.

'Look here Myra, we seem to have got off on the wrong foot which is not a good choice of words as far as I am concerned. I still have a bruise on my foot where you willfully stabbed me with those ridiculous high heeled shoes of yours.'

'Whoa, just a minute, that was an accident for which I have apologized. What were you doing skulking in that area of the house anyway?' she flashed at him.

'Skulking? I was doing the same thing as you were: looking for the loo. As soon as you strode away with your nose in the air I went in and found that beautiful Edwardian suite that so impressed you.' John replied.

When she noticed the look of extreme pain on his face, something inside her began to bubble to the surface. She laughed out loud.

'I cannot remember when I have ever had an argument over the virtues of a toilet so let us just forget that it ever happened? OK?'

John's face lit up and for the first time Myra realized that he had a wonderful smile. Her gaze lingered just long enough for him to do the same thing. After that, conversation became slowly more animated. John held the position of a Museum Curator. He told her about the days spent outdoors in the field where he collected interesting specimens as well as his passion for history and antiques. She told him about her career as a journalist. She hoped that one day she would become involved in a story that could have a great impact on her world.

Between them there grew a mutual respect. John suggested that they should visit some of the wonderful tourist locations in London. He hired a small car and they set out each morning to different destinations. Madame Tussaud's waxworks, The Tower of London, The Strand, St.Paul's Cathedral, The Houses of Parliament, Big Ben and many other sites of interest. Myra loved markets and asked John if they could visit Portobello Road.

'Why not?' said John. Notting Hill has a very colourful past and according to this brochure, Saturday is the main market day for antiques so let's go.'

Tourists and shoppers filled the market place. Myra naturally reached for John's hand as the crush enveloped them. He smiled at her with that devastating smile and kept moving as if they had always walked this way. After a while they stopped for coffee next door to a pawn shop. John took the opportunity to browse in the window. He didn't see the proprietor's face turn visibly pale with a shocked expression.

Ikey turned his back to the window, picked up his phone and called Merv

MYRA AND JOHN
LEARN A LITTLE ABOUT SPOONS

'Hey Merv, get your skinny little body down here as quick as you possibly can. I think that I've just seen a ghost.'

Merv owned a pushbike for 'special occasions' and this seemed like one of them. The door bell jangled and in strode Merv.

'Watch'er Ikey, seen any old spoons lately?

Ikey blushed as he fluttered his eyes and beckoned Merv.

'Please don't talk that way. My old girl was ready to put me into hospital after my reaction to that caper, but take a look outside at those two having coffee.'

There sitting at the table as large as life was David who bought 'his Coronation spoon,' only now he seemed to look about twenty years younger. Ikey and Merv stood silently watching this man sitting there with a pretty young woman, with confusion and curiosity spinning around in their heads.

'Ikey ave you got any idea wot is appening? That cove is so much like David that he could be his twin bruvver. Wot is he doing here? Has he been takin any interest in your shop?'

'No, don't be daft Merv. There is nothing here in the shop that could interest him. He had a quick look but he only eyes for her.'

'I asked you to come here because I wasn't sure that I was seeing right, but I now know we both have the same opinion about this blighter.'

'Well if you and I fink that he is David's bruvver, 'as David sent him to spy on you? Do you fink that perhaps he as some bad ideas abart the last business that we did ere?' Merv whispered.

'No, I don't think anything of the kind, but we had just better watch ourselves. You can never tell with people like David Collins.'

Merv made a mental note of that name. This was the first time that Ikey had revealed the surname of the cove that they had done business with and it could be an important name to remember.

When John and Myra stood to go, Merv also took his leave. After John had paid the bill, he returned his wallet to his back pocket, which was just what Merv was waiting for. An old pro at lifting wallets was Merv, and he had lost none of his skill. Carefully he hid it inside his jacket before returning to Ikey's shop.

'Well there it is, a driver's license with the name of John Collins. I seem to recall that the toffs drink a cocktail wif that name, but this certainly proves the family connection. Ikey you was right to call me. We betta keep an eye out for any trouble.

'I saw you take a quick glance in that window. Do you have any special interest in antiques?' Myra queried.

MYRA AND JOHN
LEARN A LITTLE ABOUT SPOONS

'Yes, my father has always been a collector and he taught me a little about it when I used to live here in London. We would often go looking for 'pieces' which were sometimes found in the most unlikely places. I think that he has now narrowed his interest and only collects silver spoons.'

Myra's brain was in a whirl as her face reddened and her expression went blank.

'Did I say something that I shouldn't? I don't usually have that effect on pretty women so please tell me if I have offended you.'

For a moment she gathered her thoughts weighing up her options deciding that John had the right to know.

'No John, you haven't offended me, it's just that I didn't expect you to say that. When he visited us in Australia, I showed him an antique silver spoon that I had in my possession. He was very knowledgeable and explained all about the hallmarks and that it was possibly of some value if I wanted to explore the possibility. What he failed to tell me was that he also collected silver spoons.'

'Ok, that is understandable. Then he was just a visitor and a family friend, but now he is your mother's husband, so I feel sure that there shouldn't be any need to be circumspect about his dealings. I have paid the bill, so when you are ready, we can go.'

After they had left, Merv slipped out of the pawn shop, blowing his nose in his large dirty hanky as he walked past the coffee shop. At the same time he slyly dropped the wallet onto the pavement.

When he arrived back John found that his wallet was missing, but a phone call to the coffee shop confirmed that it had been found. When he collected it the next day he was surprised to find that his cash was still inside.

The night before David and Vanessa were due to return, John suggested that he take Myra to his favourite French restaurant in Soho where the food was excellent. Despite the plain timber paneled walls and the austere décor, the food was the best that she had ever eaten. A bottle of red Beaujolais certainly helped to make it more than memorable. John drove into the garage sitting silently for a minute.

Myra turned to him saying.

'John that was the perfect ending to what has been a...' She did not get the rest of the words out. John leant over towards her encircled her with his arms and began to kiss her slowly. Myra responded knowing that her feelings for this man were something that had grown with intensity. After a minute or two John pulled away and made a move to exit from the car. Myra realised that this was possibly the best step to take, so she did the same. As they reached the front door she said to John.

MYRA AND JOHN
LEARN A LITTLE ABOUT SPOONS

'I will never forget tonight. It was wonderful, thank you. We have to make an early start to meet the plane so I will say goodnight.'

He nodded as he opened the door for her and said.

'Good night Myra, I'll see you at breakfast.'

Vanessa and David stepped onto English soil with big smiles, evident happiness and a wonderful tan. David threw his arms around his son's shoulders.

'There is a lot to be said for love and marriage. You should try it some time.' John changed the subject, mentioning that he had booked his flight back to South Africa. He was due to fly out in a few day's time but he hoped to spend some time with his Father before then. David agreed with as grin.

'That's fine as long as my wife can spare me.'

The two men did spend time with each other. So much so that for once John felt a close bond with his Dad which he had never experienced before. Perhaps his love for Vanessa had opened his father's eyes to the importance of relationships. On the eve before his son's flight David took him into his study and locked the door behind them.

'John before you leave there is something that I have to tell you. When I married Vanessa I had to change my will, but I want you to know the details, as you are my only child and we do not intend to have any more offspring.'

'Dad this is not really my business. Of course your marriage means a different distribution of your assets. I understand that.'

'First hear me out please. My happiness is such that every day spent with her means the world to me. I have left this house to her, but what I am about to show you is my legacy for you which has been tabled already in my will.'

David moved aside the picture revealing the secret cabinet and after unlocking it, turned on the light. He stood back and allowed John's eyes to absorb this collection of a few hundred silver and silver/gilt spoons. John had seen some of these spoons before but although he knew they were precious to his Dad, John's tastes were more eclectic. However he knew that this was a sizeable collection and that his Father had spent years and money in acquiring them. David took his son's silence for appreciation and he went a step further.

'I have also made arrangements that on the date of my demise you and you alone are to enter this room to remove these spoons to use as you see fit.'

'But why all the secrecy, I know that they have always been your passion but surely all this is not necessary for some spoons with a limited monetary value?'

David looked into his son's eyes then back to the cabinet before he said.

MYRA AND JOHN
LEARN A LITTLE ABOUT SPOONS

'What I am about to tell you is for your ears only. If you ever reveal it to another person, I shall deny it and remove you from my will.'

John was unsure about where this was heading and he was not happy about his Father's insinuations.

"I am telling you that I have in this cabinet a valuable spoon which is priceless. I have left the details with the identification in a sealed envelope which is in a panel behind this cabinet. That is why when the time comes only you can enter this room and only you must remove the spoons.

Recently I have had the cabinet fitted out with the latest security device known to man. If anyone tampers with it without using the correct combination, a grill will immediately drop down and seal off the shelving. At the same time an alarm will be set off at the closest police station. Even if someone manages to find this cabinet they will have little chance of removing my collection. I have had a second key made just for you and it comes with the combination that you must use to open the cabinet. I will give it to you before you leave.' They shook hands as John agreed to all of this but he thought that his Father was behaving a little oddly.

When Myra and Vanessa were looking at all the lovely gifts bought for her family, Vanessa told her daughter.

'I am so happy darling, David is so kind and generous and even though the honeymoon is over, we are going to work at keeping the magic alive.'

Myra knew that this would be the love of her Mother's life, as she hugged her with tears in her eyes.

— CHAPTER FOUR —

Risky Business

Although Merv was aware that David Collins and his son were a force to be reckoned with, he was always on the lookout for something which would return him a nice little earner, so he asked Ikey a question.

'Just say I did find another of them spoons, do you fink that someone might be interested like?'

'Ikey smiled and shook his head.

'I doubt if you could find anything to interest Mr. Collins, and Merv, I am not about to take on any more risky merchandise, so let's leave it at that.'

'Ta very much,' said Merv as he left.

Another visit to his old chum's shop in the West End was needed. There stood Peter, a picture of sartorial splendour dressed in a blue and white pin-striped shirt with a spotless white collar, a silk cravat with a pearl stick pin and faultlessly pressed navy trousers.

'Cor Peter, you certainly look the part. Anyone commin in ere would fink that he was lookin at Lord Summfink.'

'Thank You Merv, I have to keep up appearances.'

'Who am I to disagree? I want to talk abart that business that we discussed last time I was ere.'

'Oh yes, I recall that you got involved with a couple of coronation spoons and the authentication was in dispute.'

'The ole thing was very strange, but we managed to get a result. Not a lot mind but under the circumstances we got off light you might say.'

'I couldn't be of much help as I remember.'

'It went darn like this. Me and Arch found a replica of the Coronation spoon as you know. We had taken it to the Tower and swopped it for the one wif the Crown jools.' Peter was incredulous.

'How in God's name did you manage to do that? This is unbelievable. Do you know what you have done?'

Running a finger around the neck of his shirt which suddenly seemed too tight, Merv continued.

'It as been done, so there is nothing more to be said abart it. What I wants to know is ow can we be sure that the one that we took from the Tower was a replica or perhaps the reel thing?'

'As I have not had the privilege of laying eyes on either of them, it is impossible for me to answer you.

We did discuss that neither spoon had any authenticating marks on them and the man who sold his spoon to a pawnshop wanted it back.

'Yes he was a cool customer. When we showed him the one which we got from the Tower, he was really pissed off, and when we told him that his spoon was now in the Tower, he seemed even worse. After he told us that he would 'think abart it' he agreed the next day to buy ours for a fousand parnds.'

'Well you have been in a strange pickle. Damned if you do and damned if you don't. I cannot comment too much about this Merv, except to say that because neither of them had hallmarks, they could have both been replicas, but I feel that one thousand pounds seems a little too much to pay for a replica. There is one way that you could clear up this mystery by going to the Authorities in the Tower and making enquiries about the spoon in their custody. I can't really see you doing that can you?'

'Strewth, crikey no!' Merv exclaimed, as he eyed Peter's elegant dress, speech and manners.

'But you could Peter!'

'That seems an awful lot of trouble to go to just to check out the validity of that damned spoon. Even if I could examine it closely, I may have to answer some embarrassing questions. It would not serve any purpose.'

'Are you bonkers? Now that I knows the name of the bloke wot bought the spoon from the Tower we can check out that spoon that he now 'as and perhaps do another swop that would be returning a right royal profit to us if you get my drift.' Peter's eyes opened wide at Merv, but being a cautious fellow did not reach any conclusions.

'Leave it with me. It might require a method and a little muscle to thoroughly check this out. What's the name of this chap?'

'That's more like it. His name is David Collins.'

A frown came across Peter's brow. He knew David Collins and his reputation as a serious collector. If David Collins had purchased a spoon and paid one thousand pounds for it, it was definitely not a replica. After Merv left, he pulled down the blinds, took out his telephone and made a call.

'Paul, I've got an interesting package for you. Come around tonight at 9.a.m. and we can discuss it.'

When Paul 'Smith' arrived, Peter told him about his conversation with an old chum. He gave him the address where the Anointing Spoon could be found and the fact that its owner was a clever chap who would have it well hidden with the best security available.

'You will need someone to assist you. That will be the easy part.'

— CHAPTER FIVE —

Revelations

John had flown back to South Africa. He knew that he was going to miss his new family, especially Myra. A few days later, she left for Australia.

Over the breakfast table David said to Vanessa.

'In all the rush to get married and have a honeymoon, I didn't make the time to purchase an engagement ring for you. Wear something special because I am taking you up to the West End to Garrard and Co, the Royal Jewelers, where we will buy the best they have to offer.'

They both set out on a lovely sunny morning. After parking the car Vanessa took his hand and smiled into his eyes as they crossed the road. Those eyes were the last thing that she saw. David heard the car coming towards them at an incredible speed, but although he tried to throw Vanessa to one side, it was too late. She took the full force and was dead as soon as she hit the ground. David died on the way to hospital.

A witness to the horror said that the car looked like an old black London Taxi, but it moved so fast that there was no time to read the number plate. An ambulance and the police were on the scene within minutes. David had left instructions with the police that should anything untoward happen to him they should contact his son in South Africa immediately. He had also given the details for Vanessa's daughter Myra and an address where she could be reached.

A day or so later when Ikey was reading the newspaper he let out a soft whistle.

'Blimey, this is terrible news.' He grabbed the phone to ring Merv. Archie answered and told Ikey that they already knew abart it and that his dad was in a right state.

'I'm coming around to talk to him. I'll be there as soon as I can,' replied Ikey. When he arrived it was as Archie had said. Merv was in a right dither.

'All right Merv, I know that this is awful news about David and his lovely wife, but why are you taking it so personally?'

'Why? Because somefink what happened could be darn to me.'

'What exactly do you mean?'

Merv looked really scared but he trusted Ikey so he decided to tell him about his visit to his mate Peter.

REVELATIONS

'Before I spill the beans, you 'ave to give me a promise that wot I tells you goes no further.'

'Blimey, this must be serious. All right you have my solemn oath on it.'

They both spat on their palms and then shook each other's hands.

'I ave a terrible feeling that I mite 'ave caused that accident becuz I went to visit an ole friend an' tole him abart David buying our spoon.'

Ikey frowned and rubbed his forehead but he was not able to see the connection.

'How is that Merv? Even if you did tell a friend about your misgivings, that doesn't mean that he would organise someone to run down David and his wife, does it?'

'Er, I dunno for sure, but I did tell my fren that David paid us a good sum for the spoon that we nicked from the Tower and he was a little cagey about someone paying that much fer it.'

'So you think that your friend may have bumped off David so that he could get hold of his spoon?' asked Ikey.

'Maybe yes, maybe no, it all seems like a bad dream to me and I don't know what to do abart it.'

'I have given you my word, so it will go no further, but Merv if I was you, I'd take a long holiday until this all blows over. Whatever you do, don't go near the police my friend. Archie can stay with me as I can do with a little help in the shop.'

'You are a gem, an' that is good advice. I 'ave a little money saved up so I can take a trip to the seaside by train. Arch is a good lad an' he will keep an eye out for me too. I will pack a case rite now.' It was early nightfall when Merv and Archie left the house. He sat down on the station and earnestly spoke to his son.

'Arch I ave dun a few dicey fings in my day but I ave neva dun anythink vilent. I would neva agree to do anyone in and if that as been the case, it is diabolically wrong. I am glad that you are staying with Ikey. He will look after you, an' I will phone you once a week, to see how fings are going.

Ikey doesn't know the name of the cove wot I spoke to abart David, but I ave written is name down on that pawn ticket and I have posted it to Ikey this morning. E can keep it safe wif all the other pawn tickets as a piece of insurance like.'

'Ok Dad, ere is your train comin, so long and keep in touch.'

— CHAPTER SIX —

Loss

John was the first to hear the terrible news about the death of his Father and Vanessa and that it was thought to be caused by a hit and run driver. He caught the first available plane to London, arriving within twenty four hours of the tragedy. He was met at the airport and informed that as next of kin, he should identify the two bodies. To this he immediately agreed but insisted that he first unload his suitcase at his Father's flat and shower before appearing at the Mortuary.

When he arrived at the Mayfair flat, John was not surprised to see two policemen standing there. After he produced some identification, a detective informed him that they would assist in any way possible. John nodded and walked towards his Father's study with a detective in tow.

'Sir, as you can see, someone has tried to break into this wall-safe, but without any success I am happy to say. The security was so good that a grill dropped down as soon as the perpetrators began their work. At the same time a police car was dispatched so the criminals would have heard our siren and fled. The only way that they could get at it now would be to blow it out of the wall. For that reason we have set up a constant watch.'

The detective continued. 'I am also offering my condolences for your sad loss. It seemed at first that the accident was just another hit and run, but after this break in, we have to consider criminal intent.'

There was no need for John to recall his Father's conversation because he knew that these two crimes were definitely linked, but he needed to know more about the collection before he opened his mouth with his opinion.

'Thank you for that. I hate to seem ungrateful for your sympathy but I have to identify my father and step-mother's bodies before her daughter arrives from Australia. I intend to do this as soon as I have showered and changed so if you don't mind, I will ask you to leave. We can take this up tomorrow.'

As soon as he had climbed the stairs with his luggage, he found the key that his dad had given him and then came down to the study. Locking the study door, he punched in the combination on the key and waited for the cabinet to open. After a few seconds the grill slowly rose. Reaching behind the cabinet his fingers found the envelope that he was looking for. Seated at his Father's desk he opened it and read.

'Dear John, if you have to open this then it means that I am dead. I have two things to say to you. Firstly, the little time that we spent together was the best and I will always be grateful for those few days. In the past I have neglected you my only son and for this I am truly sorry. Most of my life I have been selfish and single minded. This all changed when I met Vanessa and my time with her has made a better man of me. She will inherit this house one day. It is now a house filled with love and laughter.

The second part of this letter is also very important. When I told you that I have a spoon in my collection that is priceless, I was not lying or exaggerating. It is a long story but suffice to say that I acquired it 'legally' from a couple of men who stole it from the Tower of London. Yes it is the Coronation Anointing Spoon, and as you will know from your knowledge of history is quite beyond value. For me it was the crowning achievement of my collection, but if I know you as I think I do, my collection will not arouse too much passion with you. So I am leaving it and all the others to you. I am leaving the decision also to you. There would never be enough money in the world that could be exchanged for this spoon.

Selling it would be a crime against your English heritage because its design predates Christianity. That is not to say that there would not be some unscrupulous collectors (like yours truly) who would pay anything that you would ask. I am leaving you on the horns of a dilemma, but although the way forward is not clear, the choice is up to you. Go to the cabinet and look for a spoon that looks just like all the other replicas. You will find it in the middle shelf on the left hand side. I have deliberately dipped it into a little baby oil and then covered it with some powder mixed with cocoa to make it look uninteresting. All the spoons are numbered but I have placed a tag with the number 33 around it. If you have any reservations about its authenticity, you will find my diary in the secret compartment at the back of the study desk's top drawer with the details of the hallmarks, which are only the silversmith's initials.

Be true to yourself.'

The letter was signed David. John folded it staring at the wall for about three minutes in total shock. He almost forgot his appointment at the mortuary. Should he leave the Anointing Spoon in the cabinet with all the others? Should he remove it and hide it somewhere else? Should he put it somewhere on his body for safekeeping or should he just leave it there?

John reasoned that if his Father had attempted to disguise it by using baby oil mixed with powder and cocoa, there must be still some of these products in the house. When he found the powder and baby oil in the bathroom, he loaded the entire collection on to a tray and took them into the kitchen where he sprinkled the oil over, mixed the powder and cocoa and then gently spooned it sparingly over the lot. When this was finished he placed them at random back on the cabinet's shelves. Knowing that someone had tried to steal the spoon collection after they had killed his Father, John was certain that there would be another attempt. The fact that two policemen stood outside gave him a little breathing space to make a decision about what had to be done. There were two hundred in this cabinet including the Coronation Spoon. If his combination key unlocked the cabinet he felt sure that it should do the same job locking it. After the grill dropped down John locked the study door behind him and raced upstairs to shower and change.

At the mortuary he solemnly attested to the identification of his Father. He left there with a steely resolve to remove the object that was responsible for his Father's death.

Myra knew that something was wrong the minute that two policemen came to her front door. They asked to come in and asked her to sit down before they gave her the shocking news. She let out a wail as her chest heaved with the terrible emotion, but she couldn't seem to release the deep pain which resulted in constant sobbing.

'Is there someone who could stay with you for a while?' she was asked.

'Oh, no,' cried Myra. 'I will have to stay with her. My younger sister is going to take this very hard. If I am the first to know, then I had better go to her.'

They both tried to answer the questions which Myra fired at them but although their sympathy was sincere their knowledge was limited. Myra wanted to go to Jill and when the police offered to drive her she packed an overnight bag and accepted their kind offer. Jill knew just by looking at Myra's face that she was about to hear sad and shocking news. The two policemen took the children outside to play in the back yard whilst Jill cried incessantly to the point where she almost became incoherent.

'I should have gone to their wedding. Why didn't I do that?'

'Despite the long flight, we could have taken the kids with us. I can't believe it. Both of them? Just when Mum was so happy, it doesn't seem fair.' Jill's tears flowed freely and she didn't try to stem her feelings. Both women sat with their arms around each other for some time in a numbed state until Brian came home from work. After a little while, Myra informed them that she would be flying to London for the funeral.

'Will you be coming Jill?' This question only brought on more sobbing from Jill until Brian spoke.

LOSS

'Myra you are welcome to stay here tonight because we need to discuss this when we are all much calmer. I'm prepared to take time off work and mind the kids if Jill wants to go to London.'

'No Brian' Jill replied. 'I must go. My passport is not current but as soon as I can I will follow Myra when it has been processed. I am sure that because of the circumstances, this can be expedited.'

Myra stayed the night but the next morning she explained that she had to make arrangements to fly to the U.K. and that she would do this from home. She hugged her sister, made her goodbyes and went home to do her packing. The phone started ringing as soon as she walked in the door. It was John.

'Hallo Myra, you would have heard the terrible news by now. I am so sorry that this has happened, and you know that you have my deepest sympathy. I can only ask you if and when you are coming for the funeral.' Myra tried to hold back a sob. John was so far away but there was no-one else in this world that she would rather be with right now.

'I am going to book the earliest flight available and Jill will follow me in a day or so when her passport has been processed. She really wants to say her goodbyes and make her peace. Is it possible to delay the funeral?

'If you give me her phone number I will confirm this as soon as possible. Under the circumstances, I feel sure that this can be arranged. Also please give me your flight details when you have them so that I can meet you at the airport.' John replied.

As long as these flights seem to take, to Myra this one seemed unending. Her emotions were tumbling like clothes in a washing machine. She was horrified to think that her lovely Mother was gone forever and although she hated to admit it, the thought of seeing John again filled her with positive anticipation.

CHAPTER SEVEN

John Fights Back

The plane set down and there he was. She tried to stay strong but when he held her in his arms and gave her a hug, the tears began to flow and she could not let go of him.

'I can't believe this has happened. How could someone run over a couple crossing the road in broad daylight? Have they been found yet? What is being done about it?' John gave her a little kiss on her cheek assuring her that he would answer all her questions when they arrived back at Mayfair. He had hired a car which gave him ample time to warn her about the situation as they drove to London.

'When we pull up you will notice two policemen standing on the footpath outside of the flat. This is because there was a break-in after the accident to our parents.' Myra was visibly shaken.

'How could anybody stoop so low? To rob a home after the two occupants had just lost their lives?

'There is a lot to tell you but not now and not here. After you have had a nap, a shower and a meal I will tell you all you want to know. Please believe me, you are going to need your strength to get through the next few days, and a few hours will not alter the facts.'

Myra reluctantly lay down and before she knew it she was fast asleep. The events of the last few days had exhausted her. When she finally did wake, her heart began racing as she recalled where she was and why. The shower felt good, reviving her spirit as did the smell of something cooking that was coming from the kitchen. She dressed quickly and came downstairs.

'Mmm, bacon and scrambled eggs, I'm famished.'

John began to dish out two helpings and handed a plate to Myra.

'Sit here Myra. What I have to tell you is an unbelievable story which will take some time. That is why I suggested that you rest before we tackle this problem. To begin with, I am truly sorry that you have lost your Mother as I feel the same about the loss of my own Father. Although the truth must be told it will only add to our misery. The most important fact to face is that time is not on our side and we both could be in great danger.'

Myra's head snapped up suddenly.

'What do you mean? How? Why?' John moved closer to her, took her hand in his and using his most caring voice said.

'Myra, I don't think that their deaths were an accident. There is a distinct possibility that they were murdered.'

Myra's face crumpled. She withdrew her hand, opened her mouth to speak, but the words would not come. She stared at John without understanding the true impact of his words.

'At first I believed that this was just a senseless accident but I did have some suspicions because my Father had told me about a very valuable object which he had in this house. He gave me a key and the safe combination if I ever needed to use it in the event of his death. After I was given the shocking news I hurried here for the funeral where I found that someone had already tried to steal this object, thankfully without success. That is why the police are outside as a deterrent to any more home invasion.'

Suddenly Myra began to comprehend exactly what John was implying. Again the tears filled her eyes and she quietly sobbed. He continued.

'We still have the most important duty to fulfill which is the funeral of our parents which I have managed to delay until after Jill arrives, but in the meantime we still could be the target for another attempt to steal this spoon.'

'Spoon, did you say spoon? Surely a spoon can't be worth the lives of two people. Are you sure about this?'

He sighed knowing full well that he would have to tell her everything. She was intelligent and compassionate and her life could well be in his hands.

'Perhaps I should show you exactly what I mean. Let's go into the study where I can explain what this is all about.'

Locking the door he walked over to his Father's desk and opened up the top drawer. He fiddled around until the back dropped forward where he found the diary. Myra waited patiently as John moved towards the painting on the wall. He slid it back to reveal a grill which seemed to be covering something which looked like a lot of dirty old cutlery. On closer inspection she realized that they were spoons but she wouldn't have given them a second glance even in Portobello Road.

John turned the pages of the diary looking for the explanation that he knew he would find. Before he did a small piece of paper fluttered from between the pages. He picked it up with a puzzled look. What was his Dad doing with an old pawn ticket? He took in the look of disinterest on Myra's face.

'Don't be fooled by their state. I did that for a reason. The one spoon of immense value is amongst all those replicas which I deliberately dirtied to make them look the same. The identity of that spoon is to be found in this book.'

Myra respected John's judgment but so far she was not impressed, so she waited whilst he searched for his answer.

'When you have found the right one, what are you going to do with it? If our lives are in danger from some deranged spoon collector, I vote that we get rid of it a.s.a.p. To tell the truth, I saw better looking antiques at Portobello Road that day we went there.'

Somewhere in his head a light dawned for John and he picked up the old pawn ticket from the floor.

'You might have something there because according to this ticket Dad had dealings with a pawn shop in Notting Hill. Remember where we had coffee and I lost my wallet? I think we need to pay a visit with this ticket. I hate to leave this cabinet like this, but it is possibly safe for a little time while longer until I get to the bottom of this.'

'I am none the wiser about the reason for this spoon's importance but if it is worth killing for, you had better tell me now.'

John explained that this spoon was a priceless relic which had been stolen from the Tower of London by some rogues who sold it to his Father. It was also known as the Anointing or Coronation Spoon and was an integral part of the ceremony as it was used to anoint the monarch at the time of the Crowning.

'In other words this spoon is of such vital importance that I am almost tempted to return it to the Tower myself.'

'I would caution you to think about this John. After what has just happened to your Father you would have a lot of explaining to do. I agree that it should not remain here but it seems that the safe in the wall is more than adequate to house it for tonight.'

John thought for a moment and as much as what Myra said made sense, he was not happy about leaving it in the safe downstairs and then going upstairs to bed.

'I think that I will go through them all anyway until I find it. Perhaps I can take it to bed with me and sleep with it.'

Myra laughed at this comment.

'They all look so disgusting. Let's take them into the kitchen and clean them up. Hey wait a minute. A good place to hide them would be in a kitchen drawer. My Nan did that once to hide a spoon away from prying eyes. We could put some of them in the spoon drawer and return the rest to the cabinet. In that way we are hedging our bets by not putting all our eggs into one basket.'

'You never cease to amaze me. What a good idea. Help me to pack them onto a tray.'

JOHN FIGHTS BACK

When Myra went to search for a tray, John read his Father's instructions which showed how to identify the priceless spoon. It was simple enough when you knew what to look for. The silversmith's initials were cleverly hidden in the ornate arabesque swirling designs in the bowl.

After they had gently washed but not polished them, the spoons were ready to be placed back in the cabinet while Myra mixed a few into the cutlery drawer. He made a decision not to reveal the Coronation spoon to Myra. It was not a matter of trust because he trusted her implicitly. He was concerned that if they were dealing with people who would stop at nothing including murder, Myra could not disclose any details if she didn't know them. John placed the Coronation spoon with the others in the cabinet because if by chance there was an attempt to steal it, the grill was still in place and an alarm was connected to the police station.

At breakfast John told Myra that as he felt that the pawn ticket was important, he didn't intend wasting any time in finding out. He rang the police station and told them that he wanted more security because he had to leave the house to organise the funeral. It was agreed that two more police would park outside the flat for the day, giving John some peace of mind. After dropping Myra at the Undertakers and waiting for her sad identification, they both left with his arms around her shoulders.

This was an awful time for Myra, but John's presence brought her some comfort. She was content to wait in the car while John went into the pawn shop. As he entered the shop, Ikey went pale again because he knew that this man meant business. John handed over the ticket and waited.

Ikey began to sweat and took out his hanky to wipe his forehead. He mumbled.

'Yes, what can I do for you?'

'Don't give me that mumbo jumbo. I have come to reclaim the object that is on this docket.'

Ikey recognised John and also this pawn ticket with his own handwriting on it. The address and the date indicated that it was useless to deny it.

'Er, I haven't got it anymore,' Ikey spluttered.

'What do you mean you haven't got it? This ticket means that there is something that can be retrieved on presentation of it and payment made of the outstanding debt. Isn't that how it works?'

Ikey called out to Archie just to give him some more time to think.

'Arch, bring me a glass of water and a chair so that I can try to work this out. Now let's have another look at this ticket. Do you know what it's for?'

'That is what I am asking you,' said John beginning to lose his patience.

'It could have been a spoon perhaps but I can't understand how you still have the docket because I think that the spoon was sold by the owner of the docket to someone else.'

'Now we are getting somewhere. Let us go back to the beginning and tell me slowly how my Dad still has a docket for something that he never collected and which doesn't seem to be here either.'

Archie stood next to Ikey and nodded his head. The man with this ticket must be connected to the man who was killed in an accident. Ikey had recognised John as being related to David Collins but of course John didn't know that. Ikey's business was all that he had and even though he didn't want to get Merv or his son into trouble he would tell this man what he wanted to know. If as he suspected the accident was not really an accident, it had taken the life of a lovely innocent woman who didn't deserve to die.

'A while ago a man bought a spoon to me and sold it as a replica. I gave him the cash for it and he took that ticket that you have with you. If he wanted to reclaim it he would pay me and I would give him back the spoon. But that didn't happen. The spoon sat there for so long that I thought he had forgotten about it, so I sold it to some clients of mine and wrote out another pawn ticket for them as a receipt you might say. I didn't think that the original seller would come back for it but he did. This then became complicated because when he came back for his spoon, my clients found another spoon with the intention of exchanging it for his spoon that I had sold to them. They offered it to the man whose ticket you hold and he did eventually buy it with some reluctance. That is how the ticket remained in his possession because he never actually reclaimed his original goods.'

John listened to this long winded tale accepting that it was the truth.

'Ok, what I would like to know is this: where did the other spoon come from that you exchanged for his original spoon that he left with you?'

Ikey was not too sure about going further with this because Archie and Merv might still be in some danger. Swallowing hard and hoping that it was what this man wanted to hear, Ikey continued.

'That is really privileged information but I can tell you that it was just another replica like the first one.'

'I believe that you have been up front with me so I am going to tell you something about these spoons. This knowledge could be dangerous for both you and your clients but when I have finished, we both will share a secret. It is this. The spoon that was sold to your customer by your clients is a very valuable one. I believe that some people will stop at nothing to get hold of it, but if your clients came by it honestly then they are in the clear. If they stole it or even received stolen goods they are in big trouble. I am willing to forget all about this pawn ticket as I can see how all this came about but if I do this you have to do something for me.'

Ikey was not one to look for trouble so he said.

'Yes anything that I can do. Just ask.'

'Do you have a safe on these premises? There is an item that I would like to bring here tomorrow for safekeeping. It will be totally encased and disguised and you would only have to keep it here for about a week. Could you do that?'

Ikey agreed, John shook hands and then left.

'Cor, luv a duck,' said Archie. 'I bet he 'as that spoon wot we got from the Tower and 'e wants us to keep it 'ere.'

'You could be right Arch and as we know that he knows where it came from we had better string along with him. He doesn't know that you and Merv nicked it from the Tower but he is one smart gent. He will soon come to the conclusion that I am up to my neck in this caper if he hasn't done so already.'

'I fink that I should tell Dad about this development. 'E as the right to know about this geyser sniffin around 'ere. Dad will phone tonite and I wants to keep 'im informed. Fings are hotting up.'

As John drove a patient Myra back to the flat they discussed the final details of the funeral.

'Before we arrive and I have to confer with that detective, I want to explain to you why I am taking this action with the pawn shop. Please don't think that I am a little detached about the upcoming funeral, but I know that it won't be too long before those people who were responsible for our loss will come looking for us. I am trying to stay one step ahead but I don't know who they are or where they will be coming from. I am going to set a trap at the pawn shop. This will tell me whether they are heavily involved or whether they can be trusted to help us.

Tomorrow I am going to deliver a package for safekeeping. It will not be the Coronation Spoon, but it will be a replica wrapped up in a pencil case. One of three things will happen. They will open it to check it out or someone will know about my visit and the fact that I have left something at the pawn shop, or it will remain undisturbed in the safe.'

'Aren't you putting their lives in danger by doing this?'

'It may seem a little like that but when we arrive home I am going to tell the police all about my plans to catch the murderers. As there already has been a break in at home this will not sound far fetched. This way the pawn shop will be carefully and invisibly staked out.'

'John you know when we first met, I told you that I was hoping that one day I would become involved with a story that would be a world beater? This sounds as if it might be it.'

'Maybe so but this story has not yet run its complete course. We have to come up with some way to return the Coronation Spoon to the Tower.'

JOHN FIGHTS BACK

After parking the car, John found the two detectives waiting for him. He went through a long but convincing story about his suspicions that his Father had been killed for something of special value.

'As it was not for his collection of replica spoons, it had to be for the object on a pawn ticket which was safely lodged at an address in Portobello Road. It is safe to assume that the criminals would visit the pawn shop to snatch it. This would be the ideal time and place to set a trap for these murderers.'

Both detectives agreed with John and begun to put the wheels in motion. This all seemed a little contrived but John was desperate. The stakes were extremely high and John wanted all the players out of the way and locked up before Jill arrived in three days for the funerals. Early the next morning he left with a kitchen dessert spoon in a metal pencil case, wrapped in many layers of paper and sealed in a large envelope. To this he added his Father's wax seal at both ends so that if the envelope was opened it would also break the seals. It was a crude method but it was set to catch either a crook or a murderer. Backing slowly out of the garage, he made a lot of noise in case he was being watched. Then he drove to Ikey's shop and delivered the package.

As Ikey took it he knew that this was going to be a test of faith and it was one which he was not going to lose.

CHAPTER EIGHT

The Game is Over

'Good morning Ikey,' said John. 'You don't mind if I call you that? It now seems we are partners in a way. I brought the envelope here making it clear to anyone who might be interested, but it is only fair to warn you that it is likely that an attempt will be made to grab it either tonight or any following night. There will be a stake-out in place. Two police will be hidden inside the shop and a car with three more will be parked in a side alley waiting to be summoned if necessary. I know that you are as anxious as I am to bring this business to a close so we have organised for you to go next door each night out of harm's way until we have caught the criminals.'

Ikey shrugged his shoulders because he couldn't really object to seeing this through to the end. Merv was due home today because according to him living in exile in fear of his life was no way to live, so the sooner the real villains were caught, the better. When Merv arrived back, Ikey convinced him that he had one more part to play before the true criminals could be brought to justice.

Ikey knew that Merv had given Peter the information about the spoon's owner, so now it was time for Merv to set the record straight. A phone call to Peter conveying his great shock about David's death would not be unexpected. During this conversation with Peter, Merv was to carelessly inform Peter that David's son had brought an object here to be placed in a safe. It seemed that it was the possible hiding place for something valuable. After hearing this, Peter decided that there was no time to lose so he called Paul to arrange a visit to Ikey's pawn shop. The Coronation Spoon was being held in the one place that no-one would think to look.

Paul and his accomplice decided to do the job this night. They stood on the footpath smoking and marking time until they felt that it was safe to enter the shop. The proprietor lived upstairs so it would be easy to persuade him to open the safe. Paul was responsible for the botched job at David's flat. Even when he managed to find the safe behind the picture, the grill system would not allow entry, all the spoons looked the bloody same. He regretted the need to kill both David and his wife, but they needed to be out of the way when he searched the flat. He was determined that tonight he was going to get it right.

Creeping around to the back door, Paul pulled a small crowbar from beneath his top coat and quickly broke the lock. When their eyes became accustomed to the darkness, they silently moved to the back of the shop looking for the stairs which would take them up to the proprietor. Frankie uttered a curse as his leg ran into an overturned metal stool. Swinging a torch around, Paul felt uneasy. The back rooms were empty and he hadn't found the safe yet. The next thing that happened was a loud piercing sound as the two hidden policemen blew their whistles. Paul was not intimidated, but he was not happy about a possible jail sentence. As he was already known to the police he ran for the back entrance right into the arms of three extra policemen who had just been waiting for the signal.

Frankie knew the game was up, but he was not going quietly. He grabbed the overturned stool, holding it at arm's length and began swinging it at anyone who tried to come near him. When Paul was handcuffed and bundled into the police van, the two men returned to help with the remaining offender who was soon overpowered. He cursed and struggled as he was frog-marched out of the shop. At the station they were charged and given the option of fingering their boss in return for lighter sentences. This was not forthcoming at first, but when Frankie was informed that he could be held as an accessory to murder, his attitude changed. He named Peter in exchange for a shorter term of 'break and enter,' but Paul had no such luck. Paul was eventually charged with the murder of David Collins and his wife. Peter was named as an accessory to murder. Both were found guilty as charged.

The following day Ikey returned the unopened package when John called for it. Merv had confessed to the whole caper regarding the spoons. From the day that Archie's idea blossomed until the day that they sold the spoon to John's Dad, all was explained. There was one loose end to tie up.

John had discussed this with Myra, but she asked him again.

'Are you sure that this is what you really want? This spoon could help you achieve anything that you have ever wanted in life: a life of luxury without ever having any more financial worries.'

'Yes it is exactly what I want to do. My life has taken on a very interesting turn since I met you. If somehow I misused this opportunity I would have worries of a totally different kind. This spoon doesn't belong to us, nor did it belong to my Father. It belongs in the Tower.'

When Myra knew that John hade made up his mind, she was happy to take the responsibility of returning the spoon to The Tower. She asked Merv and Archie if they would like to accompany her as they were the ones who had taken it in the first place.

It would be a fitting closure. Neither was keen about that idea.

'Blimey dad, we could be frown in the clink if they sees us again. And we did make a few trips to that place and I'm not reddy to go there again. And wot in hell is closeya?'

'Well Arch is sorta as a nice ending if you knows what I mean. Us nicking the bleedin spoon and us takin it back again. It makes me feel a lot better I can tell ya and yore mum would be so proud of ya.'

Myra grinned in spite of herself and said to them both.

'Tell you what, how about we all go together. You can wait in John's car while I go inside and give it to the Yeoman of the Guard? Agreed?'

That is exactly what happened. Myra tied a few cushions to a belt around her waist beneath a large swing coat. Wearing a long black wig, sunglasses and a floppy hat, she looked unrecognizable. She carried the magnificent Anointing Spoon safely wrapped in reams of tissue paper which John had placed inside a pencil box which was wrapped up again into a small parcel.

She walked up to the Guard, enquired about the Ladies Room, asking him to hold onto her parcel for a mo, as she was in a big hurry. Before he could object she was walking almost cross legged in the direction of the toilet. Once inside she ditched the coat, sunglasses, wig, hat, belt and cushions. It was easy to walk past the guard who didn't give her a second glance. In time he took the parcel to his superior who opened it. An expression of amazement spread across his face. The attached typewritten note explained that this was the Coronation Spoon which had been removed some 'ten years ago' and was now being returned to its rightful place. There was nor more explanation given.

That was how a national disaster was averted. The Coronation could have gone ahead with the replica and it might have never been discovered but quite a few people did know about it. They also knew that they had the power to achieve a little miracle. It was a great story that Myra never got to write about, but she had other rewards. John was one of them.

When Jill arrived the funeral could go ahead and the mourning of the death of their Mother began. John was a rock to both women, but to Myra he was more than that. The funeral was conducted with simple dignity as all knew that both David and Vanessa had found something quite rare if only for a short time.

Sitting alone with the coffin in a separate room after the service, through tears of regret, Jill came to terms with the loss of her Mother. When she whispered her goodbyes she also did a bit of soul searching. Myra had told her that she would not be returning to Australia for a little while as John had asked her to stay and help him finalise the affairs of their parents. Jill agreed but she was anxious to return to her family anyway. She was mindful of this terrible experience and how precious her own family was to her. When Myra did return they would share a closer relationship.

Ikey kept his business and his dignity. Archie went to work for Ikey where he took a real interest in 'second 'and stuff.'

A secret smile crossed Myra's face as she remembered that John Collins shared the same initials as the ones on the old silver spoon back in Australia. She knew that there was unfinished business attached to it and that the same applied to her relationship with John.

A.E. Stewart

This author began telling stories at the age of six in a Sydney boarding school. Once lights were out, tall tales were in. 'Ghost stories' were the most popular but it was the repetition of speaking and composing which produced words at a speed far quicker than anyone could write them down that started the treadmill. Such a place became the nursery where a vivid imagination was born.

A.E. lived in England for some time prior to the Queen's Coronation, where a wealth of experience with the 'Cockney' way of life and the different accents of the London population was gained.

The series of 'The Silver Thieves' was born from a younger brother's inspiration. His love of Silver and the borrowed 'Sterling Silver and their Hallmarks' book became the catalyst for this writer's literary intentions.

If you enjoyed this book, please leave a review on Amazon.

Contact A.E..................................jacana3@bigpond.com

A.E. STEWART

QUEEN'S TREASURE

The Queen's Coronation Spoon is stolen, leaving Myra to avert a national disaster.

Then in 1952 she comes into possession of a spoon stolen right from under the nose of Captain Cook himself, straight off the Endeavour in 1770.

Shrewd buyers circle, but a stubborn Myra obsessed with discovering the origin of Cook's spoon, hangs on through insurmountable challenges.

Excitement turns to disaster for Myra during the Queen's Coronation but the discovery of a cache of silver lifts her spirits; until religious fanatics ruin her honeymoon in Timbuktu.

A race against time to save the crumbling manuscripts of Timbuktu demand John's serious attention, but Myra's needs take priority as her life hangs in the balance.

The translation of the origin and the engraved message of the silver bracelets are revealed to John, but has he heard the whole story?

In the fourth century A.D. a young woman unites the nomadic Tuareg tribes of the Saharan Desert region.

Loved and known as the "Mother of us all," she is called Queen Tinan Hinan.

She commissions two silver bracelets, the engravings forming a map to the hiding place of a vast treasure.

But this connection to an ancient culture prevents anyone from unlocking the secret.